LITERATURE/
THOUGHTS

Vol.1

POWER AND
SOCIETY

GU MO-RYONG;
YOON IN-RO
TRANS:
KANG DO-HEE,
SETH CHANDLER

SANZINI

Contents

∞ Review

Σ Preface

Opening *Literature/Thoughts*

The journal *Literature/Thoughts* aims to reason on the relation between the literature—or 'literary things'— and the thoughts—or 'rational things'— ranged over the past, present and future. Slash(/), the sloping line expresses the aspects of relational power and we will endeavor to do whatever available.

The reciprocal slash of Literature/Thoughts penetrates each other, complements and translocates and also, forecloses one another. The job to discover and conjugate this relational power in the context of history can be revealed as a method of the history of thoughts, which divert the bloody history of dogma, doctrine or violence. As Maruyama Masao, the historian of thoughts who gives us the methodology has mentioned, "We always have to pay attention to the starting point of thought, the period of gestation, rather than the final results of the thoughts. That is when it is ambivalent, but bears the possibility of not knowing where it navigates."[1] The history of thoughts suspends 'the history of facts', which includes investigation and interpretation using the controlling thought police. It abscinds any annotation of 'the theory of thought', which materializes the originality of the former texts in the pretext of establishing one's arguments—or law— effectively. Therefore, we should bring into question the ambivalence, ambiguity, bilaterals, or androgyny, that are condensed in the point of creation, statement, unleash of a text. It is important to perceive qualitative criticality as the possibility[Feuerbach] of text, a vector of power. This journal *Literature/Thoughts* will cite the potential tense which 'could be' different, and re-dispose the monstrous foreign aspects that have been bitten, lacerated, and stamped by the present relation of power.

In the process of the outtake, however, the possibility of ambivalence is not grasped as genuine, linear, or secure, but always be the vertex of ex-involvement polluted by the vector of violence. The editorial of Literature/Thoughts pursues the criticism that differentiates the diabolic-

---

1   *On the History of Thought's Way of Thinking*, 1960, In the Lecture
    at International Christian University

ambiguous pollution in the disaster, hoping the tangent line adjoining the vertex. The hope can only be accomplished in the frustration with endless waits and demands. We start the journal in this faint hope. We wish and require this common sail to arrive at the decision and cast an anchor at the stationary state of the decision. *Literature/Thoughts, s*o to speak, take root in the decision and displacement of *telos*, across the board.

with a willingness to coedit,

Yoon In-ro,

Busan, June 2020

Ⅱ Criticism

Critical Notes on the Method of the Local

Gu Mo-ryong

1.

Recently published, *Three Generations of Railman*(2020) written by Hwang Seok-young challenged both criticisms that the writer has no other labor literature after *The Road to Sampo*(1973) and *The Guest*(2001), and that he only released historical novels or made a detour to allegory or fictional geography. This novel requires scrupulous reading in the respect that it originates from the local experience in 'Yeongdeungpo' and describes the family history of three railman generations across the period of the Japanese colony and the time of division. I expect the novel to surpass previous works such as *Three Generation* by Yeom Sang-Seob, *The Dwarf* by Jo Se-

Hee, and Jung Hwa-Jin's works of labor literature, but also anticipate that it may not overcome the drawback of family history novels which gained popularity in the 1930s. (I hope it just remains as my concern.)

Lee Hyun-woo, who read Hwang Seok-young as a trend of world literature, criticised him for selecting himself out to Jang Gilsan, on his way from the Vegabond Literature such as *Gaekji(*1971) and *The Road to Sampo(*1973) to Long Novel. Lee explains the literature of Hwang in the frame of creating the working class and the perspective of the novel, with the standards of world literature between the 19th and the early 20th century. How will he understand this novel, who even argued that the order of *Gaekji* and *The Road to Sampo* should be switched? Modernity symbolized by the railroad in the novel penetrates both 'mobilized modernizations' of the colony and Park Jeong-hee's dictatorship. It was during the Yu Shin (Revitalizing Regime) of Park when Hwang made a detour to Jang Gilsan. There was superincumbent political force toward National Literature, and the pressure on the working class was vicious. The way he used Jang Gilsan as a symbol of Minjung(People) is not that different from the allegory in *The Man who Left Nine Shoes* by Yoon Heung-gil and *The Dwarf* by Jo Se-hee, as an indirect response to the social situation. It is difficult to ask the writer why he does not choose 'modern long novel' without considering the context of forced modernization from above. Overlooking the circumstances of the 1960s and 1970s, when the rural dissolved and both the farmer and the laborer became the urban poor, Lee explains,

> In the history of European literature, Bourgeoisie is always depicted first, then the lower class. For us, the actual industrialization and urbanization happened in the 1960s and it became the reality that prescribes Korean society afterward. There is an advanced model here, as capitalism is invented in Europe. Balzac or Flaubert's work showed what happened in middle-class Bourgeois society during the industrialization, urbanization, modernization in the first half of the 19th century in France. The other half was shown in Emile Zola.
> Unless the decisive flaw of not stepping up to long novel, Kim Seung-ok's *Mujin Kihaeng* is relevant to French literature in the middle of the 19th-century modeling the Bourgeoisie. It cannot reach a long novel because the protagonist accomplishes the rise of his status not by his own struggle but by his wife's selection. Compared to a European novel, it seems a deflect. With the same social structure and the protagonist who is in the lower

class, we can see what happens in Emile Zola's
work.[1]

Referring to the history of French literature including
Balzac, Flaubert, Emile Zola, Lee explains the location and
limits of Kim Seung-Ok's *Mujin Kihaeng*. Without a doubt,
Lee equates the development of European capitalism,
which observed bourgeois to be the ruling class and the
proletariat confrontation, with the modernization in Korea.
However, can we see the state monopoly capitalism such
as Korea similar to the creating stage of the working class
following the Bourgeois? Here, an identified orientalism is
exposed at that the result of the comparison is obvious. If
we are still in modern times and cannot rush to observe first
and last with the tool of imitation, it is rather important to
explore what kind of literature is produced in this different
circumstance. Kim Seung-ok, Hwang Seok-young, and
Yoon Heung-gil, and Jo Se-hee are located in this Korean
situation of mobilized modernization and condensed
modernity. Laborers and farmers are the exploited class in
the seventies. "If we consider 'World Literature', Hwang
Seok-young's next novel should have been the work such

---

1   Lee Hyun-woo, *Modern Literature Class in the Wave of World
     Literature*, Seoul: Chusoobat, 2020, p.157(The numbers below
     remark the pages of citation)

as Emile Zola. It is the form of a modern long novel that responds to society so correctly that we can add meaning. Renouncing that kind of novel, Hwang returned to the historical one"(2020: 157-158). Is it true? Except for his writing style, Kim's *Mujin Kihaeng* is conventional and afterward, he turned into popular novels like writers as Jo Hae-il or Jo Seon-jak. Meantime, there was governmental projects for promoting the National Literature including the 16-volume 'Compendium of National Literature' published by the Korean Culture and Arts Foundation, mobilizing writers who had been worked since colonial times. For example, authors such as Lee Ju-hong, Jung Han-sook, and Son So-hee wrote novels about national historical figures, Gyeong Dae-seung, Jang Bo-go, and Queen Sunduk. It was this movement of compulsory National Literature that made Hwang conceive and write *Jang Gil-San* to protect Literature for Minjoong. He might have had *Im Kkeokjeong* by Hong Myung-hee in mind. It is surely a deflective and formulaic attitude to condemn the novel for the clumsy representation as a long one, with little thought of the sixties and seventies' political background. Of course, *Three Generations of Railman* is not an answer to Lee's criticism. As the writer mentioned, he intended "a long novel presenting laborers all over the surface" while offsetting the qualitative loss of the novel compared with short stories in Korean literature. In this respect, it is interesting that "Yeongdeungpo", the backdrop related to the writer's personal experience, invoked creation as a local. Nevertheless, he uses the word "province" without much consideration,

> Lee Jin-oh was released after about one month. By the agreement, it is time for the reinstatement of the eleven people who endured a long wait after the discharge. They took a bus from Seoul and visited a factory located in a province. There were a few rusty machines remained and no workers left. They also went to the old tenement house, and it has a wall crammed with moles and a plastic papered floor sunk here and there. So furious, they call the company but cannot reach the higher-ups. The staff reply that they need to wait for the new staff to be recruited and sent down. The workers laughed hollowly and sometimes fought with each other. Before leaving the place, they would share soju, the last three people looked upon the glasses not facing each other.

The paragraph needs a close reading to understand the context of the word 'province'. It is clear that the narrator or implied author uses the word as a general term without much self-consciousness. I admit the author's strategy to generalize the peripheral context of the labors, but the 'province' should have substituted for a specific region, to raise the novel's embodiment. It is not that sensible to expose the lexis framed in dichotomous thinking of Seoul and the province, if it is such a novel that "intended to reveal the root of Korean industrial laborers' present through a century of the modern era, with an eye of peripheral figures, foreigner, excluder. The structure of the Seoul-province is harmful to both. One may delude oneself feeling central calling province and social movements are no exception. I believe that the novel criticise this centralism.

2.

Author Hyun Ki-young once said, "Novelist never gets old." The remark rejects critical prejudication. Jose Saramago(1922~2010) got attention releasing *Raised from the Ground*(1980). He became an author after *Land of Sin*(1947) but spent his life as a welder, editor, translator, journalist. Still writing in his nineties, he is the standard of the ageless novelist. He would write about people in Alentejo, southern Portugal. *Raised from the Ground* is a story of three generations of farmers in Alentejo. Based on his own experience, he gradually expands the novel's sight departing from the peripheral Minjung. He takes notice of "their experience from the rough life of virtue, their austere attitude originated from the life"[2], "the obstinate, confident modesty"(162), "the imagination of the seaman who creates all places that he discovered"(164), and "the direct fury of Portuguese who were despised along with European history"(166). If I can compare, I want to place Saramago alongside Hwang. Referring to Joyce, A Portrait of the Artist as a Young Man, most of the great artists create formative narration expanding the world from the experiential and concrete life.

Here, we can take note of Arundhati Roy's recent novel *The Ministry of Utmost Happiness* because she was the one who Karatani Kojin takes as evidence of the end of modern literature. She, who turned her eyes to social movements in India sacrificing the fare with *The God of Small Things*, is a real activist noticing the limit of modern literature, so to speak, but after *The Ministry of Utmost Happiness,* it became Kojin's prejudgment.

There is an author named Arundhati Roy in India. She won Britain's Booker prize in 1997

---

2   "On How A Character Becomes A Teacher and A Writer Becomes His Student", *Father's Travel Bag*, Paju: Munhakdongne, 2009, p.160.

and became famous for the best-selling novel. However, after the award, she is busy with the movements against dam construction or war and releases essays only about those things. It is common for an Indian writer who gains popularity in America to enjoy a fancy life moving to America or England. When she is asked about her suspension of writing, Roy answers she does writing not because she is a writer, but she has something to write, and she cannot write a novel during this period of crisis.

It implies that the social role of literature sees the end. If the era of literature changing society is done, it is impossible to write or be a writer in the true sense. Then, writer is just the name of one's job. Roy does not choose social activities discarding literature but succeeds in the conventional meaning of a 'literature'.[3]

Is it fair to relate Roy to the end of literature's social role? Let us change the question. Has literature ever done a social role? We definitely need an essay with an argument for the antiwar movement or movement against

---

3   Karatani Kojin, tr. Yoon In-ro, "The End of Modern Literature", *Earthquake of Thoughts*, Seoul: b, 2020, pp.52-53.

dam construction. She lays aside novels for those real problems. It was the result of her going into the local after the Booker. Kojin interpreted this from his angle, that she choose another path giving up "a fancy life moving to America or England". It is acceptable that "Roy does not choose social activities discarding literature, but succeed to the conventional 'literature'" but her sight of literature is different from Kojin's. Either novel or essay, writing is a performance from oneself. A concrete reality in India is Roy's object of writing. It is in the First World that a novel can imagine a nation. There, Kojin includes Japan naturally and says so does Korea. It is his own explanation of 'the end of the modern literature'. However, it is incorrect because the literature in Japan, which has the "skew structure of nationalism on top of the weak society"[4] is different from the ones in Korea, which agonize the Minjok(ethnic) Literature above National Literature especially in the divided system after the war. In the same manner, we cannot consider the literary field in India the same, who just vaulted as a member of the Third World, from the periphery to the semi-periphery. Roy's remarks did not mean she does social movement abandoning novel but there were "emergent engagement" in the critical reality with no time

4   Kang Sang-jung, *Uprising Nation/Subsiding Citizen*, Paju: Sakyejul, 2020, p.9.

to write a novel. It is also true that she has never declared to stop writing a novel. (In the interview with the Guardian, she said that "There is nothing more important than a novel. It is the essence of me. I am a storyteller. For me, it is the only way to understand the world, all the gestures of the world."[5]) Moreover, what Kojin neglects the most is that her novels pay attention to the female outsider on the fringes of the world. Kojin's modern literature does not escape western and male-centered points of view. We should see the emergence of woman's fiction in a new light, whether it is in the western or non-western world. I can take Nancy Armstrong's *Desire and Domestic Fiction: A Political History of the Novel* for example. Roy's novels exist with the advent of the woman's fiction in non-western, semi-periphery society. Roy is a writer who penetrates the essence of peripherality. *The God of Small Things* is a family story set in the local, Ayemenem, Kerala, which is the writer's hometown, and she expands it to entire India at *The Ministry of Utmost Happiness*. It represents the value of justice, love, free and equality through the minority.

In "from Author" Hwang said,

---

5   Min Seung-Nam, "Hizura's Cemetery Paradise", the postscript of translator in *The Ministry of Utmost Happiness*, Paju: Munhakdongne, 2020, p.582.

Watching the chaotic neo-liberalism world, some
people say that it is time to move from global
capitalism to another order. They say it is our own
effort that shortens or stretch this period of agony.
In the time of the cosmos, our period and trace
may exist nothing but a speck of dirt. However,
I do not want to lose the hope that the world will
make slow progress.(617)

He still seems to see literature as the permanent
revolution. This is the point where he and Murakami
Haruki, who think of novelist as an occupation, diverge.
Kojin's modern literature means modern novels that had
power, to be concrete, the classical long novel from the
nineteenth century to the mid-twentieth century. During
this time, a novel creates the imaginary identity of nation-
state and represented the print media. Now as the necessity
for a novel to lead nationalism has weakened, and the
technology encompassing movies, TV, computer and
the internet develops, we can say that the modern novel
already loses their position. It reflects globalization of post-
nation-states on the other side and accepts the change of
information form(Marc Forster) after new media. This is
all related to the *Death of Literature* by Alvin Kernan who
succeed in the discourse of the end of text by Marshall
McLuhan. Why Kojin call it the end of modern literature,

not the modern novel? It is because he considers after the modern era. It will be different if we see ourselves still exist in modern era, during the progress of modern literature. There are literature of Latin America, Eastern Europe, Asia, Africa in different times of modern. Western Literature that came out earlier cannot be a model, and literature of the non-Western world that emerges later can change the map of world literature. This is all because history has not ended yet.

3.

The prosperity of modern literature is contemporary with that of orientalism. As Edward Said mentioned, "European culture attained its own power and identity by alienating the orient, which is the surrogate and concealed part of itself."[6] Sea and sea literature especially has been located in the pioneering site of orientalism. There is *Odysseia* of Homer as the origin, and *Robinson Crusoe*, *Moby Dick* and *The Old Man and the Sea* led the history. Some suggest Islamic adventures of sea and purification from the 7th to the 13th centuries(Masakatsu

---

6   Edward Said, *Orientalism*, tr. Park Hong-kyu, Kyobomunko, 1991, p.17.

Miyazaki, *World History of Sea*), but it is hard to change the hegemony. Sinbad in *The Arabian Nights* is also sea literature, but not strong enough for denying the superiority of the western in a sense of global capitalism. Then how can we deal with the sea literature? We can point out the upsurge of marine economy and empirical realism. Think about the genetic local method, not the way to compare texts transcending time. When we catch the emerge of marine economy and realism, we can understand the aspects of modern far from the periodical order. Although it is not literature, Dutch genre painting, is a sample of this genetic method.

In *Eloge of the Quotidian*(tr. Lee Eun-jin, Seoul: Puri&Ipari, 2003), Tzvetan Todorov focuses on genre paintings describing quotidian life, which cover the social and cultural changes from religious art to secular art. Andre Malraux said, "Dutch paintings contrived not the way to put fish on the plate, but the way not to make the fish food for disciples". Among the art painting people, Todorov assesses that genre painting gained unprecedented status past portrait and history painting. It paints anonymous folks. It refuses the tradition of a familiar story. It chooses themes among all behaviors creating human life. Therefore, in the 17th century, in the Netherlands, not the heroes in religion or myths but the daily life of anonymous people became a central subject and aesthetic for the first time.

Todorov's attention reaches realism to describe the daily scene. Individualism and realism are linked. Individual motive and volition are important to depict realistically. Realism overwhelms allegory. The word realism came from the 19th centuries but it is right to explain Dutch paintings.

It is also associated with Ian Watt's appropriation of realism to the rise of the novel. The desire to represent the experience of new facts makes Defoe write *Robinson Crusoe*. It is when maritime novel emerges, a new style not to repeat the familiar narratives like tragedy or epic, so maritime novel in the 18th century inherits the genetic tradition of sea painting and genre painting in the 17th century. Sea painting is the result of realism in relation to the cultural change of oceanic transition, the growth of the marine economy in the 16th century. After the life following continual moral norms, the life adapting to transgression and contingency and targeting new value and object emerges. The desire to record new experiences and transitions is expressed in painting.

Sea painting and genre painting reflect the maritime modernity in the 17th century, Netherlands. Todorov points out that genre painting was formulated above the maritime economic structure. That is why after the 17th century, the significance of Dutch genre painting did not show up. Todorov remarks, "the genre paintings on the daily life of Dutch is present in a moment of history." The tradition of realism art from this time is inherited only through technic and motif. "The admiration, joy, love of daily life" disappeared. Why "the essential thing" as he said, never come again? After genre painting, realism devotes itself to agony, frustration, and melancholy. It runs parallel with the descend of the wealth of the 17th century's Netherlands above the maritime economy.

Robinson Crusoe of Defoe is a result of empirical individualism and realism based on the maritime economy and capitalism in the 18th century England. It was a new form in both aspects of perception and structure. We can see "the characteristic of relation between economic and religious individualism and the rise of the novel".[7] However, still in the genealogy of maritime novel, Herman Melville's *Moby Dick* is a whole new style of novel. As Nathaniel Philbrick explains, who wrote nonfiction *In the Heart of the Sea* tracking the story of Ship Essex that provides a backdrop for *Moby Dick*, "Melville did not write the book only with his own experience in the Pacific, but he was absorbed in reading records of the whale fishery and Pacific."[8] The novel is a result of the desire to inform

---

7   Ian Watt, *The Rise of the Novel*, tr. Kang Yu-na et al. Seoul: Kang, 2009, p.125.

8   Nathaniel Philbrick, *Why Read Moby-Dick?*, tr. Hong Han-byul, Jeonyuguichaek, 2017, p.11.

the study of nature by empirical individualism. He also included the reality of American society. Therefore, it became the novel about a voyage to Pacific for whaling and more about the America careering to Civil War. Again, the novel floated to the surface of the maritime economy accumulating the capital by collecting the whale oil. The whaling ports, Fair Haven or New Bedford in Massachusetts. is important backdrops. There is also Nantucket Island where the whaling industry started.

Then how can we explain the birth of Korean Sea Literature? When is Korean marine conforming to the Western modern marine that escaped from the Mediterranean? When, so to speak, was the 'oceanic transition' into the Atlantic, the Pacific, and the Indian? Karl Schmidt categorizes the Atlantic on the coast. It is not before the emancipation, since the Eastern/Asian Atlantic were blocked by Japanese Imperialism. In the late 1950s, deep-sea fishing vessels were departing, and in the 1960s, merchant ships led import and export in Busan. As the desire to proceed to the ocean, Cheon Geum-seong and Kim Seong-sik's sea novel and sea poetry emerged. Compounding empirical individualism and realism, sea literature was developed with the economic high tides. Our emancipation was that of the ocean. Trapped in the sea of the Empire, the route toward the ocean opened. Busan was the topos practicing the real meaning of this emancipation.

Though it started as the colonial city made by the Japanese Empire, without the oceanic city Busan, it must have been hard for Korea to modernize or economically develop. Based on the maritime economy of Busan, Korean sea literature has been produced inheriting empirical realism. The local interacts with the world.

4.

Franco Moretti's *Distant Reading* is a way to discover world literature.[9] It can also be a way to filter national literature. However, it premises translatability, and as it subject to linguistic performance such as English, Spanish and French, it does not diverge from European centralism. If we consider the politics of untranslatability,[10] we should refuse Morettis' world literature. Casanova's theory on world literature brought Bourdieu's literary field into the reality of world literature.[11] She thinks a phenomenon in a country occurs on a world scale like a fractal. She also overlooks the untranslatability and shows French or European centralism as she prescribes Paris as the capital of

---

9   Franco Moretti, *Distant Reading,* Verso, 2013, pp.3-4

10   E. Apter, *Against World Literature,* 2013, pp.3-4

11   Pascale Casanova, *The World Republic of Letters,* 2004

world literature. Then what about constantly close reading the literature of one's country? If the literature from other countries keeps translated and dominates the market, will it fall the possibility of the literature of a country? It is a difficulty of untranslatable periphery literature. Murakami Haruki's works, for example, could also be written assuming the translatability.

The progress of Local Literature study at the national level has been repeated steps. While it restructures the National Literature or Minjok Literature continuing historical investigation, Critical Localism is perceived as an important writing technique. Here, 'local' features a space-creating new value. It is not a symbol of marginalization as it was in the past, but a position to make a new creation possible.[12] A local area is a place where tradition and modernity, coloniality and modernity, culture and nature are mixed, and putting the ambivalent values together, creates new values. With the prospect of global capitalism beyond the national standards, Critical Localism maintains its rationality by motivating self-criticism and fulfilling the criticism of the other. Like a fractal, the global structure of the central and the peripheral also appears in every region in the world. Critical Localism assumes those regions as places that can transmit new thoughts, and relates the

---

12   Dirlik, *The Postcolonial Aura,* 1997, p.85

history and performance at the level of the local area to the reform of the national social system, even to the demand for a change of the global system.

Im Woo-ki suggested 'Basin Literature', from the concern that "Local Literature premises the subordination to the 'main literary world'" and he sets the association of adjacent regions as "the local condition of the concept 'basin'".[13] He explains that the area that has similar nature and economic background, common language, and same culture/tradition can be other basic conditions for the basin. Also, he includes ethnicity, so that it "converges into the Dialect Literature and expand to the World Literature" and deals with main agendas like "mutual culture", "remembering the history of people's death". It is a method focussing on the "individuality and originality" of the Local. There remain problems about affection between regions, nations, and the world, or consideration about (un) translatability, but I think it is a meaningful concept as it is linked to Critical Localism.

Interviewing with twenty-two world-famous authors, Eleanor Wachtel found that they are perceiving and focusing on "the essence of peripherality".

13　Im Woo-ki, "Basin Literature", *Today's Literature with Cinema*, 2019 Fall, p.44.

I already realized that a writer's life, like ours, is created by their relationships with parents, siblings, lovers, and children. One thing I found, however, is that the most common and often appearing feature of writers is the peripherality, the status of a stranger. In such a position, though it may entail pain or loneliness, most of the authors value the status of a stranger. Because the standpoint and authority to see the world of an author come from that position. Ironically, we can understand the world that they are showing because of their peripherality.

(…) This kind of irony—the essence of the culture is discovered by the peripheral writing—is important to many writers.[14]

The meaning of the exilic vision that Said has said, is examined by writers' specific statements. The background of creation shown by world-famous writers is not central. They perceive their location as local. The local is a place where empirical life is situated. In this local, nation, ethnicity, and the world are present in various forms. Orhan Pamuk says, "writing and literature remind me something

---

14   Eleanor Wachtel, *More Writers & Company*, tr. Heo Jin, Seoul: Xbooks, 2017, p.17.

deeply related to a deficiency, happiness, and guilt in the core of life."[15] Authors should be cautious about the fantasy that they are in the center. If they are at the center of society, they can tell the violence and deficiency of it. In this point of view, the local is a way of writing and thought. Oe Kenzaburo said, "the basic form of my literature is departing from the personal problems and relating it to the society, nation and the world."[16] It is followed by the idea that it "seeks to the healing and reconciliation of human with the prospect of someone located peripherally." Gabriel Garcia Marque also said, "if we cannot put in practice the legal support on the people who live by the imagination of owning their life at the periphery of the world, the European who rules our dream by their standards will make us lonelier".[17]

It is not just about the poiesis. Gayatri Spivak suggests "teleopoiesis meaning copy and paste" as "an ordinary technique of new comparative literature."

Aristotle could get away with saying that imaginative making—poiesis—is a better

---

15 Orhan Pamuk, "Father's Travel Bag", *Father's Travel Bag*, tr. Lee Young-gu et al., Paju: Munhakdongne, 2009, p.66.

16 Oe Kenjaburo, "Unclear Me in Japan", *Father's Travel Bag*, p.211.

17 Gabriel García Márquez, "In What Perspective Shall the World see Latin America", *Father's Travel Bag*, p.267.

instrument of knowledge—philosophoteron—
than istoria, but I cannot, especially since we
live in a time and a place that has privatized the
collectivities imagination and pitted it against
the political. Begin to see that all poiesis is
teleopoiesis, I say above. Think that eventuality
as a task, even as a persistent institutional task "to
come."[18]

It is quite difficult to clarify, but I understand as an
assert that it is the power of imagination not reverting to
ethnicity or nation but crossing the time and space that
should be an important concept of writing and criticism. It
is different from the way Kojin perceives Arundhati Roy.
As Spivak said, it is important to recognize the globality
instead of globalization, and in this point, the position of
Roy's *The God of Small Things* and *The Ministry of Utmost
Happiness* is clear. Globality requires teleo-poeisis and
the method of the local to meet teleopoetic imagination of
globality through the specificity of the local. Of course, to
confirm this issue, it is necessary to read texts carefully.

18 Spivak, Gayatri, *Death of a Discopline*, Newyork: Columbia
University Press, 2003, 37-38

The Sea as Mythic Space:
The Possibilities of Choi In-hun's Sea

Kim Geon-u[1]

"The breadth of the possible. That decides everything."[2]

1. The Sea and Choi In-hun's Literature

The meaning of the Sea to Choi In-hun is very special. *The Square (Gwangjang)* begins with the oft-quoted first line, "The sea breathes with a heavy ruffling of its bulky, blue scales, more vibrant than pastels," and ends with the lines, "The shadows of the white seabirds can't be seen. Not on the mast, nor on the nearby sea. It seems they left

---

1   Kim Geon-u is a doctoral candidate in sociology at Bielefeld University and German correspondent of *Kyosu Shinmun*
2   Choi In-hun, *A Dream of Utopia (Yutopia ui Kkum),* in *Complete Works of Choi In-hun 11*, (Seoul: Moonji Publishing, 2010), 198-199. [All translations are the translator's unless otherwise noted. — Translator's note]

for some other place in Macao."[3] This cycle beginning and ending at the sea takes on an ouroboros-like self-referential form with no start or finish. Just like self-reference, this form, figured in the image of the sea, not only provides a figuration for infinity but also evokes emotions of the infinite. The sea, containing within itself the watery horizon which always postpones arrival, thus including itself within itself, is also the most potent of symbols. The sea—for which the transformation of the self is the maintenance of the self, the event of the self, and the state of the self.

Speaking about his novel *Headword (Hwadu)*, which he formulates as a 'self-reflexive novel' continuously experimenting with and exploring form, Choi In-hun once said that the final place of literature, the final destination of the novel, is the recollection of what one has said until now: "It's like putting a big mirror in the place of the drawing model and drawing oneself instead. In the mirror you would see yourself drawing, right? In other words, it's a novel written about oneself writing."[4] *Headword* is

3   Choi In-hun, *The Square/The Nine Cloud Dream (Guunmong)*, in *Complete Works of Choi In-hun 1*, (Seoul: Moonji Publishing, 2018), 25, 209.
4   Choi In-hun and Yeon Nam-Kyung, "From 'Tumen River' to 'Letter From the Sea,'" *Meditations on the Way (Gil e Gwanhan Myeongsang)*, (Seoul: Moonji Publishing, 2010), 403-4.

a novel written with a clear self-consciousness of its self-referential form as reaching an extreme of literature, and the author describes it as 'a seafarer's log,' its path one of the author tying himself to the 'mast' of literature to ride out the tempest. In this way, *Headword* is a project that questions, in the form of literature, it's own coordinates, the coordinates of literature, and the coordinates of Koreans as free, modern humans. Of course, "because the ship is ultimately in the sea, and not in the captain's quarters,"[5] these are moving coordinates, coordinates always at risk of running aground, and moreover, coordinates which always contain within themselves the possibility to change. While *The Square* begins and ends on the sea from two different perspectives, *Headword* takes a conscious self-referential form in which start and finish coincide. The first lines, "Flowing forever and ever over 700 *li* to reach this place, the Nakdong River gathers its branching waters into one body and heads out to sea," are the same as the last, "Flowing forever and ever over 700 *li* to reach this place, the Nakdong River gathers its branching waters into one body and heads out to sea..."[6]

5　　Choi In-hun, *Headword 1*, in *Complete Works of Choi In-hun 14*, (Seoul: Moonji Publishing, 2014), 10.

6　　Choi, *Headword 1*, 23.

And the last lines of *Bridge in the Sky (Haneul ui Dari)*, which has its fiftieth anniversary of publication this year, are "Before the unknowing sea. Before that idiotic blue-green beast. Not knowing, I mean, who is responsible for the traceless disappearance of the family members who disembarked the LST here on this sea. Listen up, I want you to tell me!" As might be expected, it is here, standing before the sea, that the painter protagonist Kim Jun-gu, coming ashore in Busan, can start his story reminiscing on his life in the intervening time.[7] Writing his perspective on art, in part as art theory and in part as a theory of fiction, *Bridge in the Sky*'s protagonist Kim Jun-gu puts his meditations down in a letter to his friend Han Myeong-gi while looking out at the sea. "The sea is the sea all of itself. It is an unevolved animal. All the large animals on this earth have gone extinct, but the sea alone lives.··· Or maybe its not that the sea does not evolve, but that it was always finished evolving from the start. It's family tree would be simple. Beginning and finish, its prehistory is its civilization, its ancestor is itself. It seems people in the past thought that way too, about themselves," he writes, facing the sea from a cultural-historical perspective. The sea's ancestor is its

---

7   Choi In-hun, *Bridge in the Sky/Tumen River (Dumangang)*, in *Complete Works of Choi In-hun 7*, (Seoul: Moonji Publishing, 2009), 138.

own present self, and with its start thus being its finish, it is the archetype of self-referentiality and autological self-containment. His observation that "I too came from the sea I suppose. When I stepped off that LST onto the shore,"[8] is thus another way of saying that he too is fated to return to this sea. What form, what method, what path is necessary to this process, with neither start nor finish, of returning to the self from the self.

Moreover, although it is not well known, *Baby Whale (Agi Gorae)*, one of Choi's two children's books,[9] is worth considering. While the baby whale of the title leaves the sea to soar through, to journey, to live in the sky, we meet with an author who represents the sky and even the cosmos in the image of the sea. It can be viewed not only as a

---

8   Choi, *Bridge in the Sky/Tumen River*, 136-7.

9   The other is *Suni and the Sparrow (Suni wa Chamsae)*. Choi's daughter Choi Yun-gyeong has discussed *Baby Whale* in an interview, reflecting that, "The sea in which the whale lives resembles the sea of Lee Myeong-jun [*The Square*'s protagonist]. My father said he always felt the viewpoint that Lee Myeong-jun commits suicide was a brutal interpretation, and that he wasn't throwing away his life but going in search of his family. He put that feeling into *Baby Whale*. *Baby Whale* is the children's version of *The Square*." "Soseolga Choi In-hun Mangnaettal Choe Yun-gyeong Ssi Soseol Useumsori Nonhajasyeossneunde Beolsseo 1 Jugi," *Maeil Gyeongje*, July 22, 2019.

children's version of *The Square*, but—in relation to the sea—as an expansion of the sea itself.

Finally, viewed in this light, it doesn't seem like a coincidence that Choi's final piece of fiction, published in the December 2003 issue of *Yellow Sea Culture (Hwanghae Munhwa)*, was "Letter from the Sea (Bada ui Pyeonji)." Moreover, from his hospital bed on July 23, 2018, shortly before he passed away, Choi repeated once more his formalization of *Headword* in "Twentieth Century Individual (20 Segi ui Gaein)"—one of the multiple prefaces written for *Headword*—as a 'seafarer's log,' a 'mast.' As if reading from his final testimony, Choi on his hospital bed described the life of Korean Peninsular modernity throughout the twentieth century, and its future fate, as 'Odysseus' Voyage.' This phrase became the subtitle of a massive collection of research on his work which was published immediately following his death.[10]

Taking the paradox in which even denial of the self

---

10 These events are recounted by Bang Min-ho, who describes Choi's work as a "record of an anguished, solitary voyage atop a 'shipwreck' in the middle of the sea, looking for a place to drop anchor, pushed by the waves but struggling to hold the rudder." Bang Min-ho, "Preface," in *Choi In-hun, Odysseus' Voyage*, (Seoul: Epipani, 2018), 7.

becomes the self as a constitutive principle of its being, the fate of the sea resembles that of literature. No, it is literature that resembles the sea. Because of the artificial medium that is language, literature is simultaneously both in and of itself realistic, and also forced to deny reality in order to become art. It is because of this paradox, which can be called "the tragic antinomy that is the fate of literature,"[11] that literature resembles the sea. However, the sea's fate is not tragic. In the words of Kim Jun-gu, the sea is the sea in and of itself, and because the sea is itself the sea, the potentially tragic element is neutralized. This is the reason that even if everything else were to disappear, the sea alone would remain. How can literature, with it's tragic antinomial fate, persist—like the sea—through constant self-transformation

---

11   "Writing a piece of literature is an act of criticism on the society in which the author lives, in the form of a struggle with language and the author's consciousness. Thus, it is the flash that arises when the author's freedom strikes against reality, and the reality of the author is a fight within language. [...] Language becomes a transparent passage to reality, and the author is in this way bound to the earth. Because language is itself a tool to be utilized by a community, the literary artist, who has chosen language, is already participating in that community's reality. The question is what stance they take in participating. And the intimacy with which literature participates is not comparable to, for instance, music." Choi In-hun, *Literature and Ideology*, in *Complete Works of Choi In-hun 12*, (Seoul: Moonji Publishing, 2009), 37.

into the self? Here lies the artistic and realistic meaning, with reference to the intellectual history of civilization, of Choi's literary world taking the sea as its environment in this way.

2. *Baby Whale*: The Sea as Space and the 'Sea of Stars'

At a memorial for Choi In-hun on the one-year anniversary of his death, his daughter, Choi Yun-gyeong, described *Baby Whale* as the children's version of *The Square*. Just as Lee Myeong-jun's decision is not one of throwing away his life but of choosing a different life path, a life that can be different, in order to live the future in the present, following an ideology of love,[12] *Baby Whale* is not

---

12 In "Love and Time (Sarang gwa Sigan)," the author's note for the 1981 play *Hansel and Gretel (Hanseu wa Geuretel)* as it was performed at the 2009 Seoul Theater Festival, Choi writes, "The Hansel and Gretel of this play beat fate through the love they share between them and a time of waiting. I wanted to present this boy and girl, taken captive by the modern witch of politics, with the gift of freedom, if only in this imaginary space-time." Choi In-hun, *Meditations on the Way*, in *Complete Works of Choi In-hun 13*, (Seoul: Moonji Publishing, 2010), 383. For the portion that views 'love and time' as the 'alternative to the colony,' see, Choi In-hun, *The Gray Man (Hoesaekin)*, in *Complete Works of Choi In-*

the story of the titular 'Baby Whale' as an orphan bereft of
both parents, but of Baby Whale heading out on a different
life path among the 'sea of stars,' where the possibility of
reuniting with Mother and Father Whale remains uncertain.
As can be seen from Choi's 1983 short story "The Moon
and the Boy Soldier (Dal gwa Sonyeonbyeong)," on the
rare occasion that Choi takes a child as his protagonist,
he is not interested in speaking out on the inhumanity of
Japanese Colonial domination or the horrors of war from
the viewpoint of the 'boy soldier' of the title. To borrow
his words, "although it was a child's story, it was even
more so an adult's story."[13] *Baby Whale* is of course not
only unrelated to typical children's story narrative with
cliches like "A long, long time ago..." or "...lived happily
ever after," but took no influence from it at all.[14] Nor is it

---

hun 2, (Seoul: Moonji Publishing, 2008), 12. For the 'time beyond
time' of "Letter from the Sea" which overcomes the 'love and time'
of *The Gray Man*, see the following interview with Yeon Nam-
Kyung, Choi and Yeon, "From 'Tumen River' to 'Letter From the
Sea,'" 422-23. There is no space for a detailed discussion here, but
in order to interpret Lee Myeong-jun's choice, one must consider
the following statement by the author: "He was overwhelmed by a
hallucination. If that direct moment had been avoided, he may well
have lived." Choi, *Meditations on the Way*, 199.

13   Choi, *The Gray Man*, 48-49.

14   In the sense that, in the case of literature, even without writing
directly, reading itself can serve as a sort of youthful writing

practice, Choi considered all of his reading experience prior to *Tumen River* to be a single process of writing practice. Choi, *A Dream of Utopia,* 334. One year before his death, Choi was interviewed for what would officially be the last time by the historian Jeong Byeong-jun. In this interview, responding to the question of which authors or works he liked most or had the largest influence on him, Choi said that while writing *The Square* he, "had no knowledge of Korean literature. Even as a reader, I had no knowledge of it at all. I of course knew nothing of Yi Kwang-Su, and hadn't ever covered any of the 1910s novels now treated as basic in literary histories. I had no personal academic connections to literature, no friend who was familiar with modern Korean literary history, no working author I could reasonably look up to as a teacher." College junior Lee Myeong-jun, whose "heart thumped like he'd read the first letter of his crush's name every time he saw the *D* at the beginning of *Dialektik* in some book," takes pride in having not a single monthly magazine in his bookshelf which was "everything to him," around four hundred books without a single work of Korean literature or even a book about Korean literature. Choi, *The Square/The Nine Cloud Dream*, 46, 51; Choi In-hun and Jeong Byeong-jun, "The April 19th Movement and *The Square*," *Yeoksa Bipyeong*, no. 126, (Spring 2019), 116. In response to a question in an interview with Kim Hyeon about what books meant to him prior to his debut as a writer, Choi said, "Books were always the one place I could go to find consolation, and feel some sort of strength and hope, and that mentally guaranteed a future life, and all that sort of thing. That's what I think." In the same interview, Choi also responds to a question about whether he was reading any Korean poets at that time: "It's truly a strange thing to say but, no, there weren't any poets from our country." Choi In-hun and Kim Hyeon, "Explorations of an Artist in Changing Times," *Meditations* able to include the process of adversity that it portrays as the opportunity to present a complete narrative, or take any influence from such a simplistic worldview. Unlike animals, humans do not receive unmediated influence from their environment, but have the potential and capability to expand their environment themselves. Simply stated, even in this children's story, Choi is interested in our world, in which a one-to-one relation between words and signs, action and environment, is no longer possible. The issue here is how we as modern people can obtain free subjectivity.

The pastoral outlook that emphasizes Baby Whale's orphanhood, having lost its parents, or suggests Baby Whale can only live happily if it becomes a good little whale and listens to Mother and Father Whale from now on, fetishizes our standardized customs, and refuses to problematize the methods for making reality into reality in the multi-layered complex of reality, or to question the legitimacy of these methods. To borrow a phrase from Kim Dong-in, Baby Whale wants to escape from the world of

on the Way, in Complete Works of Choi In-hun 13, (Seoul: Moonji Publishing, 2010), 68-70. The following research is also worth consulting, Jang Mun-seok, "Thinking in 'Our Language,'" in Choi In-hun, Odysseus' Voyage, (Seoul: Epipani, 2018).

'bearing a resemblance in the toes.'

Baby Whale begins with Baby Whale's wish: "Dad, I want to fly through the sky."[15] Mother and Father Whale respond, "If whales could fly they wouldn't be whales," and "Everyone knows whales can't fly," and ask Baby Whale "Why would you want to fly through the sky when you can swim and play in the pleasant sea?" Mother and Father Whale are living in the world of 'bearing a resemblance in the toes.' They are living by the customs of life in the sea, and the natural order of being a whale. To them, a 'wild rumor' that whales can fly is not even a rumor, but merely noise. This is the point at which Baby Whale can be read as *The Square*'s Lee Myeong-jun.[16] To borrow the narrative of *Shoo-oo Shoo Once Upon a Time (Yetnal Yetjeok e Hweoeoi Hweoi)*, a child born to a hero's fate, as in the rumors of hero myth, can be thought of as murdered by the order of tradition. From this viewpoint, the world of customs, without any basis of legitimization, exercises murderous

---

15   Choi In-hun, *Baby Whale*, (Seoul: Samseongdang, 2004).

16   "Living listening to wild rumors is a sad way to live. We meet our fate when we stop being satisfied with rumors and go see for ourselves. Let's call the place where we meet with fate 'the square.' The rumors about the square are various. What I'm trying to tell you here is the story of a friend who was not satisfied by the rumors and decided to go see for himself."

violence, in the sense that it steals away a person's life. Ignorant of the strength and violence of such customs, Baby Whale claims "the sea is boring." Baby Whale wants to fly through the sky so badly that it can accept the possibility of never seeing its parents again. Then that night, like our tradition of 'exactly three times,' Baby Whale wishes three times, "Even if I never see Mom and Dad again, I want to fly through the sky."

And at that moment Baby Whale breaks free from the world of custom and soars through the sea of stars. As the sky becomes the sea, the stars become sea rocks, and from the stars grow corals, and big flowers bloom on big stars, and small flowers on small stars. As it swims between the moon and stars as in the sea, and drinks the stars and spurts them out like in the sea, "Baby Whale frolics amongst the sea of stars until early morning, flying through the sky." As the sun rises, Baby Whale wants to go back home, to the sea where its mother and father are, but no matter how far it flies, the sea where they swim is nowhere to be seen. That night, Baby Whale, who now wants to return home, asks the stars about the sea where its parents live, but none of the stars can answer, and Baby Whale loses interest in the stars, and in flying through the air. Crying, Baby Whale calls out, "Mom! Dad! Come take me home. I promise I won't fly through the sky ever again," but no one responds, and the stars in the endless sky just twinkle indifferently. In this way, "Baby Whale flies on. Above the sea of stars. Without knowing where to. Unable to know when it will return to the sea of its mother and father." Concluding the children's story, the author leaves the future open, asking, "Will Baby Whale ever be able to find the sea where its mother and father are? Will Baby Whale ever meet Mother Whale and Father Whale again?"[17]

Because this children's story does not guarantee that Baby Whale will ever meet its parents again, or that Baby Whale will safely return to the world of custom, it is a sad story. At the same time it is a scary story, not only because of the matters of life and death, giving and taking away involved in the stealing of life that resembles hero myth, but also because of the horror brought on by loss of direction. This can be called the "terrors of anomy."[18] It is the fear the author expressed when he said, "Twelve years ago, I built a diver named Lee Myeong-jun in the workshop

---

17   Choi, *The Square/The Nine Cloud Dream*, 20.

18   Peter Berger, *The Sacred Canopy: Elements of a Sociological Theory of Religion*, (New York: Anchor Books, 1990) 90. Berger states "To be in society is to be 'sane' precisely in the sense of being shielded from the ultimate 'insanity' of such anomic terror." Berger, *The Sacred Canopy*, 22. Following Berger's logic, Baby Whale is subjected to anomic terror because it craved the outside of society.

of the imagination, and sent him into the sea of life.···
Just as we must begin life without knowing what it is, the
novelist must send the protagonist down into the depths of
life without ever knowing what life is. If the protagonist
comes back alive then we hear the sad and frightening story
of those sea depths from their own mouth, and in the case
they don't return, we come to know the depth and fear of
that place that begins where contact was cut off." Seeking
direction in an unknown direction, continuing to swim
despite not knowing if it will be able to return home, Baby
Whale is the 'diver' of the sea of stars. Baby Whale will
experience the depth and fear and sadness of life. However,
coming to terms with custom would mean, in the words of
Baby Whale, 'boredom' in place of the fear and sadness.
Not knowing where it goes, Baby Whale will continue to
soar above the sea of stars. The place where it will live
is not the natural order of the sea, but the sea of stars, the
limitless fantasy space of the sky. As will be discussed later,
this reveals that fantasy and reality are not in contradiction,
and this children's story is beautiful in that it depicts a
concept of reality in which fantasy is a reality-within-
reality which constructs reality. Baby Whale must now
follow its own path and seek a deep, mythological meeting
in the mythic world of the sea of stars. The sound of Baby
Whale making its own path while living a reality-within-
reality will become the sounds of the waves and of the sea

of stars. That story will become Baby Whale's 'letter from the sea.'

In this way, the sea is a sad, frightening, beautiful space.

3. Metaphysics of Resurrection and a Mythic Meeting: "Letter from the Sea"

This sad, frightening, beautiful space is, more than anything, a deep space. The experience of 'depth' when encountering the world of Choi In-hun can most readily be confirmed in the deep space of the sea. When Choi writes "The problem is one's self. One must always return to the self. All abstract nouns are like a wide public square,"[19] it is the sea that can be read as that wide public square. But because this wide, deep public square called the sea contains all the many gradations between the abstract and the concrete as a part of itself, it is both realistic and conceptual. As a multi-layered complex, it requires a 'spiritual sight' which can track and explore the depth and breadth of reality. In the question "Simplicity is not

---

19 Choi In-hun, *A Day in the Life of Gubo the Novelist*, in *Complete Works of Choi In-hun 4*, (Seoul: Moonji Publishing, 2015), 103.

sufficient; nor is diversity. Where is the sorcerer who knows how to make an alloy of silence and oratory?" the sorcerer is not a sort of hero or charismatic character, but the space where the 'alchemy of silence and oratory' unfolds: the sea itself.[20] "Letter from the Sea," too, is contained within this image of the sea, and when Choi In-hun describes the meaning of this image—"When I write 'the sea' of course it means none other than 'the sea,' but this contains an inexhaustible multitude of meanings. The sea is the sea, and also it is human, tree, flower, and elephant. It must be able to transform with endless freedom following the viewpoint of the reader."—this sea is the sea as a space where the 'alchemy of silence and oratory' unfolds.[21] On the other hand, in the sense that "'On the waves there are nothing but waves.' The sea has no character, in the original

20 For a more detailed explanation, see Kim Geon-u, "Mythological Encounters and Us – Choi In-hun's *Bridge in The Sky* and the path of Self-identity," *Munhak gwa Sahoe*, (Spring 2020), 362-69.

21 Choi In-hun, "Portrait of the Artist in the Northern and Southern Dynasties Period," *Meditations on the Way*, in *Complete Works of Choi In-hun 13*, (Seoul: Moonji Publishing, 2010), 355-56. Moreover, in relation not only to "Letter from the Sea," but on the character of literary works in general, Choi prescribes a 'reading technique' of revealing "the layers hidden within the depths," in other words an "act of becoming the speaker oneself." Choi, "Portrait of the Artist in the Northern and Southern Dynasties Period," 354-55.

sense of the word, which comes from the Greek *charassein*, meaning to engrave, to scratch, to print. The sea is free,"[22] the sorcerer called the sea can, according to it's abilities, be described as freedom itself.

However, there is a difference between the sea being freedom and perceptions of the sea being freedom, and the ability to identify self-identity through the sea, remember freely through the sea, and freely connect multiple selves through the sea is not the sea itself, because the sea is freedom itself. It is not a problem for actions in reality to fall short of an established ideal standard, for example freedom as the criterion of an ideal order; on the contrary, this difference is the 'human condition' for acting in reality. It is not possible to make decisions or choices without doing so. Nor is it necessary. In reality, a person cannot go on thinking, continuously observing, forever. Instead, "Taking action in reality, wherever the line is drawn, is only possible when this conscious reflection has ended. [...] It is self evident that realized actions will display some deviation from an ideal standard. Every civilization has means to correct this deviation after the fact. These

---

22 Carl Schmitt, *The Nomos of the Earth in the International Law of the Jus Publicum Europaeumi*, trans. G.L. Ulmen, (New York: Telos. 2006) 42.

are institutions like opposition parties, scientific research, art, religion. These are activities that realistically and symbolically compensate for the difference between reality and ideology."[23] As one of these institutions, literature, too, is an art form made possible by the existence of this deviation. The sea, because of its depth, demands a conceptual thinking through of this deviation, requires conceptual observation and description of it. Therefore, a metaphysics of the sea is necessary.

In an important interview on "Letter from the Sea," Choi emphasizes the depth of the sea by repeating that it 'keeps going down.' To take a rather lengthy quotation from this interview: "If you go down beyond the oceanic current of history · society to the current of anthropological life, and down beyond that to the sea floor of metaphysics, the measuring weight naturally keeps going down and down to the universal condition of the human.⋯ I wrote this, this feeling of steady descent through sociological reflection, historical reflection, political reflection, in a sort of seafarer's log, a measurement log." Of course, the

---

23 Choi, *Meditations on the Way*, 190. The expression of this within literature is, "Even still, it is never possible to extend the preparation for writing forever, and at some point one must begin to write. In other words, it can never begin from anything but an imperfect state." Choi, *Meditations on the Way*, 170-71.

metaphysical condition of humanness which Choi finds running through the history of civilization is refugee consciousness. This is true in the sense that, "Humanity itself is a being excluded from something, humanity itself has fled to this universe from some conflict."[24] When human universality is confirmed at the depth of the sea floor, the condition of humanness is not simply limited to the biological body. This self in excess of the natural body is conceptual in that "when it attempts to be accurate even about things it has not directly experienced, through thought, an ability unique to humans, it takes an unexperienced, unseen and unheard [...] result which exists concretely before the eyes in the present under the name reality, and responds by describing it."[25] This is a conceptual action, and takes the form of memory crossing back and forth across the distinction between the self and not-self. Choi, explaining that *Headword* makes memory the central symbol of crossing back and forth over distinctions, says that "memory in this case is also love, and also revolution. I had this in mind as I was writing,"[26] and it is in this sense that 'crossing back and

24 Choi and Yeon, "From 'Tumen River' to 'Letter From the Sea,'" 421-22, 425.

25 Choi, *Meditations on the Way*, 189.

26 Choi In-hun and Kim In-ho, "On Memory," *Meditations on the Way*, in *Complete Works of Choi In-hun 13*, (Seoul: Moonji Publishing,

forth across distinctions' is used here. In other words, it is not an erasure of distinctions or a claim of not knowing the distinctions, but on the contrary, civilizing the distinctions, at once sharpening them and softening them,[27] and in doing so making more various distinctions. In this way the act becomes a metaphysical one.

In "Letter from the Sea," the speaker—"something like a loose coalition of myself," the 'I' that was once 'I'—longs for its old body, becoming a 'we' and then an 'I' with the statement, "we feel I." But soon, that 'something like a loose coalition' becomes neither 'coalition' nor even 'something like,' and "at some point, a time difference has formed amongst this unity." It is a skeleton, lying spread over a space many times the size of a typical human body, at the unknowable depths under the sea. Eventually each of its parts becomes completely detached from the others, and it realizes that it will become "some sort of ambient sadness

2010), 332.

27 "In this life consisting of the impermanence of all things, the strongest and wisest of things is soft movement. In this life one must have a soft heart, if only to endure the sadness of being separated from someone you once loved. [...] The first condition of finding happiness for modern humanity is to rediscover the soft heart that can sever the cycle of undesirable deeds." Choi, *Meditations on the Way*, 131.

turning and swirling around my selves." Feeling that 'I' am soon to enter into a new form of being, "it seems that it will be difficult to maintain the singularity of my memories, my reminiscences," and as the thing which had previously secured the singularity and unity of 'myself,' those "memories even now are starting to change slightly."[28] The structure for the self-observing consciousness noting these changes to adhere to has already disappeared from the ribcage and arm and leg bones long ago. For all that time, the skeleton is watching and perceiving the slight displacement of the bones, wavering amongst the seawater and fish, the shadowy light that reaches down into the deep sea, knowing that all of these memories will disappear, all of these reminiscences will dissolve into the seawater. And at that time "those memories of a time when I was not the fish, and not the sea, nor even the light, will no longer belong to myself that has become the fish, become the sea, become the light."

The skeleton, knowing that it will soon become the sea, writes a letter to its mother in the moment of its last memory, saying it was a young person who, "once the hideous gash of the armistice line was cut, began crawling

---

28 Choi In-hun, "Letter from the Sea," in *Letter from the Sea*, (Seoul: Samin, 2012), 512.

beneath the dark crescent moon in a tiny submersible like a flatfish minnow," having been assigned the "special mission, the especially dangerous mission of conducting reconnaissance in a submersible on the maritime frontline."[29] In this speaker, whose father is on the other side of the armistice line, who is recalling the special fate and historical disharmony shared between two countries, it is not difficult to see a reminder of *The Square*'s Lee Myeong-jun.[30] Considering the thesis of the abstract noun as a wide public square, and that the 'skeleton' itself is an abstract noun—a singular, but wide, public square—it is possible to generalize its meaning. The skeleton is at once Lee Myeong-jun, and Choi himself, and the hideous gash of the demarcation line, and even further down, it is every Korean person of the twentieth century who knew and lived that line as fate,[31] and ultimately every modern person. This

---

29 Choi, "Letter from the Sea," 515.

30 For Choi's own words on Lee Myeong-jun and the history of the division, see Choi In-hun, "*The Square's* Lee Myeong-jun, Recollections of Frustration and Anguish," *Meditations on the Way*, in *Complete Works of Choi In-hun 13*, (Seoul: Moonji Publishing, 2010), 177-93.

31 "In the skeleton, the individual memory and systematic memory first suggested in *Headword* are harmonized. The anonymity of the 'skeleton' makes it possible to include every individual of the Korean people who lived through this generation." Because of this abstractness, the skeleton soon becomes one with the sea, and with

is an expression and image of self-reflection which, after passing through the biological level, the political level, the sociological level, and the historical level, has finally arrived at the metaphysical level.

With its memories steadily dislocating to match the number of its disintegrating bodies, "Myself lying about here and there. Myself scattered here and there" finds itself in a more severe situation. "Instead of dissipating as a single ego, the young mind gradually disintegrating in the sea becomes a kind of divine shaman, hearing all the sounds in the world in 'a roaring flood.'"[32] That roar, "screamed

---

the sound of the waves. Yeon Nam-Kyung, "The Literary Revival of Memory," *Choi In-hun: A Writer Interrogating Literature*, (Seoul: Geulnurim, 2013), 171.

32 Kim Myeong-in, "Literary Last Words of an Eternal Border Dweller: Choi In-hun 'Letter from the Sea,'" *Parting with the Self-Evident*, (Seoul, Changbi 2004), 230. For Choi's comments on this work during an interview, see Choi In-hun and Kim Myeong-in, "A Society of Perfect Individuals," *Meditations on the Way*, in *Complete Works of Choi In-hun 13*, (Seoul: Moonji Publishing, 2010), 345-46. On the topic of this 'divine shaman,' Kim Myeong-in cites the poem "Sea Battle (Haejeon)" inserted into the 1962 novella *The Nine Cloud Dream*, and Yeon Nam-Kyung, in addition to "Sea Battle," points out the thirteenth chapter of *Bridge in the Sky*. Kim Myeong-in, "Literary Last Words of an Eternal Border Dweller," 233; Yeon, "The Literary Revival of Memory," 172; -Choi and Yeon, "From 'Tumen River' to 'Letter From the Sea,'"

from all four corners of the sea's depths," "like boxes inside boxes," "like wrinkled flesh, calls up memories." 'Like boxes inside boxes' the sound is further amplified until it becomes "the wail of the vast sea." The time most apt for this sound is not day but night. Whales twist under the weight of that roar. "A flood of sounds calling out in the night. I lie at the bottom of that massive flood and listen to its sound. The roar of the flood is too loud. The too loud roar is soundless."[33] 'I' become something other than 'I,' stray thoughts that belong to some unknown others flow into 'myself,' and all of this is "frightening, sad memory."

However, it is also 'I' who discovers yet another 'I' equipped with a 'surprising memory replay device.' On that day sometime far in the future, we will have evolved into a humanity capable of overcoming this frightening, sad story, and can move beyond the strength of this desperation. The strength to move beyond paradoxically arises in the dissipation of the present 'me' and the beginning of a "long march for resurrection in the everlasting future," to become 'myself' again in distance future days. 'We' and 'I' must first begin to disappear in order to be reborn. And this is nothing other than "constructing words." The earth

---

419.

33   Choi, "Letter from the Sea," 518-19, 532.

becomes a line of poetry, the earth becomes words, and in order to understand the earth's words, "to construct words as large as the earth, the poet drinks anti-sleep medicine." However, construction of words is not the exclusive possession of the poet. If the 'I' who can comfortably call out to 'Mother' can transform into someone else's words and travel around, then anyone can begin a 'long march to resurrection.' "Until we meet again."[34]

Just as the 'boxes inside boxes' amplify the stray thoughts of the sea, inside 'the selves within the self' we meet with a larger version of our self. This is also "the connection of many selves, the thing we lump together for convenience in 'I,'" and then "one realizes that the being one thought of as the self is really nothing more than a shadow, and the true self is some sort of mythic being." It is the discovery of the self as the protagonist of myth. The reason that Lee Myeong-jun is the protagonist of a myth in the world of Choi In-hun is not that he lived a mythic life, or that he provides us a mythological model. Myth is "not the story of a special person, but the name for the life of a regular person who lives deeply."[35] Through the mythological meeting of 'you' as another 'me,' 'I'

---

34   Choi, "Letter from the Sea," 523, 525.
35   Choi, *Meditations on the Way*, 121, 123, 133.

become 'we' in one sense, but at a metaphysical depth, 'I'
am having a mythological meeting with 'many selves.' At
some point 'I' myself, watching and being conscious of the
'I' writing the letter under the sea, become the wide public
square of an abstract noun.

As a deep space, the sea is a sad and frightening but
beautiful space. As all these spaces, the sea is to Choi an
'abstract noun' and also an abstract place, and in that sense
it is, as pointed out above, a neutral space. It is then that
the sea becomes a metaphysical space that can sing of
resurrection.

4. Sea Sounds: The Complex of Contingencies and Sounds of a Mythological World

When we perceive the sea, we are open not only to the
visual dimension but also to the auditory. It may even be
better to say that we are exposed to the sea, in the sense that
the sea embraces us as an environment. The sea is the cry of
Lee Myeong-jun's seagull and the waves crashing as they
roll in and out, and in that way it is the sound of repeatedly
making and erasing borders, and the sound of sand and
pebbles which form one part of the sea meeting with the
sea, their own larger self. The sound of the sea always

overflows, so just as it begins to disappear as a momentary conception, just as that conception begins to fade, it is immediately heard again. The sound of the sea not only wanders about our vicinity like a phantom, but also as a sort of medium, surrounds us with the ever present possibility of taking a form.

Here its worth taking note of Choi In-hun's essay "At the Sea (Badatga eseo)." The sound of the sea surrounds him as "a sound that can be heard but remains inscrutable," but causes him to sense its distance from the self. This is because "The sound of the sea overflows inside me. Everything inside me is submerged inside it. That everything—my home, the city, my studies, the people, the back alley of a distant country—those things are the sound of the sea."[36] In this way the sound of the sea is the sound of disparate things, things without a point of commonality, mixing. In a unity of polyphony, the things absorbed by the sound of the waves are in neither conflict nor contradiction. Rather, in the sense that they may be different from each

---

36 Choi, *Meditations on the Way*, 157. This idea appears in another variation in "Letter from the Sea:" "A skeleton cannot love, graduate, get a job, go to the library, read a book, or listen to music. Even if it wanted to know and to do so many things. The living will do the things I wanted to do, I'm sure." Choi, "Letter from the Sea," 516.

other and are neither inevitable nor impossible, they are
contingent, and given that structure, they form a "complex
of contingencies *(complexio contingens)*."[37] The place
where the self-deconstructing skeleton of "Letter from
the Sea" sends off its letter to Mother—at the last moment
before the connections of memory detach—is, of course,
the sea. And the letter itself will be the sound of the waves,
and the skeleton's mother will answer with yet other wave
sounds.

Here the sea sounds, the sounds of the waves, become
'stray thoughts.' The sound of the waves, always different,
and yet always 'there' all the same. A sound without
meaning, that can say whatever it wants in 'that place.'
The stray thoughts that are the sound of waves do not
discriminate between thinking too much, or thinking too
complicatedly, or not thinking at all. This indiscriminate
sound is always in that indiscriminate space, 'there,' all
the same, but differently. Listening to the sounds of the sea
at the seashore, Choi says that life requires a hole where
one can listen to this sound. This hole which must not
be lost, which is in fact the form that makes life into life,

37 Niklas Luhmann, *Soziale Systeme*, (Frankfurt: Suhrkamp, 1984),
52; Niklas Luhmann, *Kongtingenz und Recht*, (Berlin: Suhrkamp,
2013), 61.

suggests that the sea is a space of some sort of excess. This autological construction of excess—which makes every contingency its own while still taking as itself the very possibility of becoming its own self—is the sea.

This autological construction of the sea can also be termed, to borrow Choi's phrase, "self-reflective continuous self-identity." Choi's definition of 'continuity' includes both the horizontal aspect of a sort of "physical inosculation"—"When a river flows, the water flows without any break in both its upper and lower parts. from the source until when it enters the ocean. No matter whether the river is as long as the Tumen or the Yalu. That is continuity"—and the vertical aspect—"What boundary is there between above and below in the depths of the sea? For the sake of convenient measurement we might talk about an upper and lower level. But the sea itself doesn't have any boundaries between above and below, does it? That's how we can conclude that it has continuous self-identity."[38] Through this imagery of the sea, the sea takes

---

38 Choi and Yeon, "From 'Tumen River' to 'Letter From the Sea,'" 413-414, 419-420. Because *Headword* was concerned with the 'depth' and 'continuity' of the sea and served as an attempt to actively chart and forge a sea route through these issues, the alternate titles Choi considered for the novel included 'Survey Vessel' and 'Icebreaker.' On this topic, see the above interview,

on a mythological meaning.

Through distinction between the layers of the self-as-nature, the human self, the scientific self, and the self-as-fantasy, self-identity is stratified into a multi-layered 'self-diversity.' As can be seen in Choi's "Three Forms of Human Metabolism (Ingan ui Metabolism ui 3 Hyeongsik)," nature, knowledge and science, and fantasy—in other words 'biological identity,' 'civilizational identity,' and 'artistic identity'—retain an autonomous self-diversity while constructing self-identity. Here, fantasy is "the state of maintaining the contradiction of the self and the world as a contradiction, while also transcending self and world," and "art is the technique of self-consciously operating this state."[39] This avoids denying the possibility that the wires of self-diversity could get crossed, and instead affirms this as the operating principle and occasion of existence itself. The relationship of self and world is a relationship of the self with itself which re-enters the self as a relationship of self and world.[40] Within that self of re-entry is a confused

---

Choi and Yeon, "From 'Tumen River' to 'Letter From the Sea,'" 516.

39 Choi In-hun, "Three Forms of Human Metabolism," *Meditations on the Way*, in *Complete Works of Choi In-hun 13*, (Seoul: Moonji Publishing, 2010), 284-294.

40 There is an interesting passage in *Headword* which expresses this

mixture of the biological self, the cultural self, and the artistic self. This is a coexistence of each self in the horizontal dimension as well as an achievement of depth for each self along vertical layers. In this way, fantasy is not separate from reality, but a reality-within-reality which constructs reality.

This sea for which the transformation of the self is the maintenance of the self, the event of the self, and the state of the self, possesses this fantastical reality within reality, this realistic fantasy within fantasy, this fantastical fantasy within reality, this realistic reality within fantasy, in the form of a 'reality-within-reality.' This re-entry form of the sea is a mythological world. The depth of the sea can be read as the depth of this reality which contains within itself so many diverse forms of reality as to include even fantasy. To Choi the sea is this reality itself and also a symbol of this

---

through the image of the matryoshka doll: "The wooden dolls are painted with vibrant colors but these porcelain dolls were painted blue and white, like all the other porcelain in the store. A doll within a doll within a doll within a...a self inside myself inside myself inside...the universe outside the milky way outside the solar system outside the earth outside Korea outside Seoul outside my house outside myself outside myself outside myself outside...the self looking at the doll inside myself looking at the doll inside myself looking..." Choi In-hun, *Headword 2*, in *Complete Works of Choi In-hun 15*, (Seoul: Moonji Publishing, 2012), 578.

reality's self-transformation. And because there are waves on that sea, we can hear the sound of the sea, and write a letter to the sea, and that letter can once again become a 'letter from the sea.' The letter from the sea is also a letter to the sea, but because we who write the letter will all one day become its addressee, the sea, it is a letter written by the sea as well. The sender and receiver of the letter from the sea are one and the same.

Thus, the baby whale of *Baby Whale* and the skeleton calling out to its mother[41] in "Letter from the Sea" are one. This is because, to borrow once more the words of *Bridge in the Sky*'s Kim Jun-gu, the sea is 'finished evolving from the start, at once its beginning and end,' 'its prehistory is its civilization, its ancestor is itself.' The cries of Baby Whale in search of Mother and Father Whale, the cries of the skeleton calling out to its mother in its final moments,

---

41 "Mother, right now at this point when our next meeting is such a long wait away, even if in the meantime my cries may become the sea and the stars and the wind and the leaves or even, like the stray thoughts crawling around in my consciousness, transform into the words of some other person who doesn't even know me, won't those cries still be the one name I can now call out vividly, 'Mother?' That's why I call to you. Mother, you can't hear me, can you? That's why I call out without inhibition. Mother, I hope you are well. Until we meet again." Choi, "Letter from the Sea," 525.

all become the sound of the waves. And the self which observes and records this, the self observing that self, the self observing that observing self's disintegrating consciousness, the self again conscious of and observing that observation, the self whose memory of those observations is dissipating, the self attempting to record and remember those dissipating things, the memory of all of this, all becomes one in the sea. The sea as a mythological space.

5. The Sea as a Mythological Space

The sea is a horizon we face on the one hand as primitive, and on the other as civilized humans. The sea is a space which provides a single outlook over the vast size of a great number of possibilities, and as a combination of the customs and methods to realize those possibilities, it is a field of action for the unfolding of ideas in history and reality. The sea, as "the tension that exists between method and custom," is a space that requires a set of coordinates and a point in time in order to realize the ability of subjectivity.[42] In this way, the sea is a space which provides

---

42 Choi, *Literature and Ideology*, 183. Kim In-ho puts this more succinctly: "It is not possible to achieve modernity without

a single outlook over the expanse of possibilities called
the future, but at the same time also overcomes anxiety
about the uncertainty of future time, as a sort of 'time's
time,' a fantastical and infinite space where "absolute time,
metaphysical time, time beyond time, a kind of fantasy
time" unfolds. However, to the extent that this infinite
space is also a place for the self-experimentation of an
unresolvable and unreachable humanity, it is a space which
demands an interior 'civilized ritual of becoming primitive'
on the part of the civilized human who experiences
anxiety and fear.[43] Here this 'civilized ritual of becoming
primitive' is another name for art, and art faces the sea
as fantastical space and an artistic reality. As a space of
'time beyond time' and as a 'complex of contingency,'
the space of the sea is more than a mechanical complex;
it is a space of greater excess and surplus than that. In
this space, history becomes reality, a greater number
of possibilities are maintained, and of those some are
realized in forms of civilization. The 'civilized ritual of
becoming primitive' becomes a sort of ideology about the
sea. However, when civilization expands, it never reaches

'conceptual modernity.'" Kim In-ho, *Narrative of Deconstruction
and Resistance: Choi In-hun and his Literature,* (Seoul: Moonji
Publishing, 2004), 40.

43   For more on this see, Kim, "Mythological Encounters and Us," 380-
81.

infinity but instead sees the horizon of infinity recede. In this way the sea-horizon[44] is the sea's horizon. The sea-horizon is at once the symbol of unreachable infinity and the boundary of possibility for all the conditions unfolding and developing there, and their historicity, to become reality. It is the horizon of possibility for the development of reality, within reality, as fantasy. It is for this reason that the sea can also be described as a medium with the potential to become a 'form' in and of itself.[45] As a result, the sea contains a reality in which the finite and the infinite mutually constrain each other in a self-constitutive manner, or contains this reality—as a reality-within-reality—as fantasy. As shown by "Letter from the Sea," the sea which the self-deconstructing self is in the process of becoming is a symbol for the metaphysics of autological, self-referential being. And of course the headword of *Headword*, namely 'subjectivity' as the problem of memory—the issue of the

---

44   [In Korean the word used to translate the theoretical term 'horizon' means literally 'the line formed where land and sky meet.' There is a separate word for the horizon at sea—here translated as sea-horizon—and no word which describes both as a single phenomena. The original therefore relies on this wordplay between the term '(land-)horizon' and the 'sea-horizon.' — Translator's note]

45   For a sociological treatment of the difference between medium and form and the problems of meaning production that follow from it see Niklas Luhmann, *The Society of Society (Sahoeui Sahoe)*, trans. Jang Chun-ik, (Seoul: Saemulgyeol, 2014), 61-80, 229-243.

subject's structure as developed solely from the connections between memories—attains meaning in the form of self-referentiality. The deep meaning of Schmitt's point that "on the waves there are nothing but waves"[46] can be understood in the context of the self-referential metaphysics of the sea in Choi's writings.

Although there are nothing but waves upon the waves, or because of that fact, there needs to be a path over the waves. Of course, because it is a path over the waves, it ultimately becomes the waves again. In the sense that it disappears as soon as it is realized, this path is an 'event.' The waves and the path over them as event, along with the sea-horizon as horizon, are excellent imagery for the metaphysics of autological being. When Lukacs claims, "The double meaning of the frontier [border] is that it is simultaneously a fulfillment and a failure [resignation]," Choi's metaphysics can not in that sense be called, like that of Lukacs, a 'metaphysics of tragedy.'[47] On the contrary, this border (*Grenze*), as a kind of difference that is a distinction of inside and out, this side and that, is a form,

---

46   Schmitt, *The Nomos of the Earth*, 14.

47   Gyorgy Lukacs, *Soul and Form*, trans. Anna Bostock, (New York: Columbia University Press, 2010), 198. [Words in brackets approximate the author's original translation into Korean. — Translator's note]

and a form cannot itself realize its own unity. Considering this point, form is not something which must be read in the first place as tragic, and instead the incompletable unity of form must be read as continuously developing and unfolding new possibilities alongside form. This form sets the sea in motion with waves rippling across it, and creates paths across the waves. This is what it means— when viewed in terms of its surface, the waves—for the sea to be a medium which needs form. Form is not so much 'simultaneously a fulfillment and a resignation' as it is a force which produces a surplus that makes 'greater fulfillment in resignation' or 'greater fulfillment because of resignation' possible. "A life without fantasy cannot be called a human life. Where there is fantasy, there is a path. Reality, step aside! Fantasy is coming through! You are nothing but reality,"[48] a path for fantasy. This path for fantasy, along which fantasy is 'coming through,' is seen in the sea. This form of the sea, as a fantastical space, is in this sense not a form for a tragic metaphysics, but for a metaphysics of resurrection. Here, subjectivity becomes a kind of myth as it attains historicity, and the sea with the form of a metaphysics of resurrection becomes a mythic space.

---

48   Choi, *A Dream of Utopia,* 198-199.

When Choi says, "That which opens a path to every person's possibilities. This is true 'breadth.' The breadth of the possibile. That decides everything,"[49] the sea is the space of not only that breadth, but also the depth which maintains it. In this self-referential space, being is generated, constructed as subjectivity, and disappears as self. This space, containing in its depth not only the accumulation of memory but also memory's roaring sound, makes the history of numberless paths of possibility its own. The sea becomes a mythic space in accordance with the depth of that history. In this mythic space, what history will we trace across the waves as we pass? And what kind of path can the path we trace be? The sea is a space of freedom, so its breadth of possibility is the 'principle of unlimited choice.' As in *Baby Whale*, this unlimitedness can engender 'terrors of anomy,' and we may have to become a new 'diver' in its depths. A diver may explore beneath the sea, but in the mythic space of the sea's depths the diver may also in the name of fantasy explore the universe. After the god of fate has disappeared, in the modern period when the god of wandering appears, even the gods may experience a loss of direction. "The form of life can always become an amorphous blob, and when the anarchy of life reveals itself without medium in that way, other names

---

49   Choi, *A Dream of Utopia,* 198-199.

for the anarchy of lost direction brought on by this are the 'sadness of civilization' and the 'fear of civilization.'"[50]

However, the sea which faces us with such sadness and fear is bounded by a sea-horizon. While an animal may simply stop when faced with the horizon/sea-horizon, humans, the "animal which takes the limit of the senses as a symbol of the real," are drawn to the sea-horizon. The sea-horizon, as "the scenery which both opens and closes the human field of vision," becomes the horizon of form's unfolding and development.[51] The developed paradox, the deparadoxicalized paradox, like the unreachable sea-horizon, becomes once again the unity of form. This is how, in the sense of a unity of difference, the paradox of form develops the incompletable unity of form into a new form. Amidst the unfolding of this horizon, new possibilities are produced, and a variety of possibilities of negation are made present, become an event, as a single difference, in a single form. Taking the limit of the senses to be a symbol

---

50 Kim, "Mythological Encounters and Us," 380.

51 Choi, *A Dream of Utopia,* 204. Choi also uses this metaphor of the 'horizon' while explaining art through the difference in techniques of continuity and discontinuity. For example: "Even if it is art created with the methods of realism, if it is art, at the end of that continuity there will be a wavering horizon with only direction and no content." Choi, *Literature and Ideology,* 145.

of the real—this is the self-development of the horizon which is at once closing and opening. It is the strength to negate the fear that comes from the depth of the sea and the sadness of civilization, and the potential to live the sea as a space of freedom which autologically contains the logic of resurrection. If modernity is understood as a "spirit of negation,"[52] this is no different from a logic of resurrection which seeks to prepare a new path out of sadness, anxiety, and horror through the possibility of new actions.

The sea is a symbol which contains as it's horizon the sea-horizon where the paradox of form self-develops. A symbol of unreachable infinity. As a metaphysical abstract noun for this sort of infinity, the sea is a paradoxial space in which self-negation is also self-legitimization and self-resurrection. The autological and self-referential sea which contains fantasy as a 'reality-within reality' is a medium where the axis of 'dream' and the axis of 'reality' appear and disappear as they intersect. Here too is confirmed the

---

52 Choi, *Literature and Ideology*, 34. This spirit of negation becomes possible under modernity only because the "conditions of equality" have been generalized. The occasion of negation does not so much become a foundation for self-indulgence as arise from an attempt to locate one's legitimacy in humanity itself. On this subject consult, Alexis de Tocqueville, *Democracy in America* (*Amerika ui Minjujuui)*, trans. I Yong-jae, (Seoul: Akanet, 2018), 49.

similarity of the sea and literature, in literature's 'tragic antinomial fate' of having, because of the medium of language, to both be realistic and at the same time, deny reality in order to become art. The sea is a space of reality and a medium that can 'make real,' but it is also a space of fantasy in the sense that it is a mythic space. And, just as it is a scary and horrifying but also beautiful space, as seen in "Letter from the Sea," its antinomial fate is tragic, but also suggests the possibility of resurrection.

6. Each Person as a Sea: Indicators of Self and the Size of Possibility

Realizing this possibility of resurrection and expanding the size of that possibility requires an 'indicator' of some kind. Choi views the entrusting of this problem to something else as a 'gamble' and argues that, in the modern world of multiple competing indicators, "inference is the only indicator to guide judgement. The value of inference increases with the number of indicators used, and to the extent that the conclusion is asserted within the parameters of the chosen indicator."[53] As conditions constantly change in the modern world and shift in accordance with

---

53   Choi, *A Dream of Utopia,* 184.

circumstances and the division of individual areas, the actions appropriate to those conditions must also be made differently possible. In other words, not only must the contingency of action be made possible, but a greater number of contingencies, like the 'value of inference,' requires a greater number of indicators. Here, for the sake of contingency of action, its not that indicators must be removed, but that they must on the contrary be made to react more sensitively to more detailed and delicate conditions, and must in this way be able to process external data. In the sense that there is only one political king, but an unspecified number or kings of literature, "The world of art is not a world of bureaucracy. To oppose bureaucracy in all forms—that is the new and eternal literary principle." In these words spoken by Mr. Gubo (of *A Day in the Life of Gubo the Novelist (Soseolga Gubo Ssi ui Il-il)*) can be read the fate of forever having to seek out new indicators. Literature must be a continuous antidote and complementary principle to the schematization of life, and oppose the solidification of any schema. It can be said, "The thing which resists 'schema' is not 'non-schema' but a 'better schema.' Art can be called, without regard to its enactment at the present moment, the 'most excellent schema,'"[54] and the schema, non-schema, better schema,

---

54   Choi, *A Day in the Life of Gubo the Novelist*, 310.

and most excellent schema mentioned here all take the form of the self-negation and self-resurrection belonging to the paradoxical space that is the sea.

Because humans are not objects, the instance of self-negation offers the possibility of self-realization. Humans maintain self-identity and construct new realities by negating reality, and enact reality's self-establishment by unceasingly searching for indicators in order to expand the possibilities of resurrection. In this way, when the possibility of negation is expanded, and when the surplus possibility unrealized in action becomes a condition of interiority, interior subjectivity is obtained and expanded. In order to make this interior surplus not shared by animals and objects into 'event' through the contingency of action, a certain 'perspective' is required. Through this perspective, humans produce a difference with their environment, and ascertain a space of interiority where the possibility of "working to gather information about the environment and afterwards convert this information into song"[55] develops. When this perspective is obtained, self-identity is maintained and subjectivity is constructed with interior surplus as the condition of being. In addition, this

---

55   Choi In-hun, *The Moon and the Boy Soldier (Dal gwa Sonyeon-byeong)*, (Seoul: Moonji Publishing, 2019). 540.

means that instead of differentiating value hierarchically—
in the sense of the supremacy of fiction over reality—
multiple perspectives and multiple indicators make it
possible to view the multi-layered complex of reality as
deeply as possible. This perspective views the modern
interior conflict and anomy, in which a greater number of
possibilities, a greater number of life values co-exist and
collide with each other, as a condition for the possibility
of the logic of resurrection. It is a mythic perspective on
the world. It negates the bureaucratization of life, and
through this mythic perspective a 'better schema,' the
'most excellent schema,' makes it possible to turn a greater
number of fantasies into a greater number of realities-
within-reality, and through this process the surplus of the
contingency of action is civilized. The quote I have used
as the epigram of this essay—"That which opens a path
to every person's possibilities. This is true 'breadth.' The
breadth of the possibile. That decides everything"[56]—
takes on significance in this way as part of the history of
civilization and the history of ideas.

As "Letter from the Sea" deftly reveals, the self is the
sea, and the sea is the self. This is the case in that, to borrow
the words of *Bridge in the Sky*'s Kim Jun-gu once more, it

---

56   Choi, *A Dream of Utopia,* 198-99.

is both prehistory and civilization, and its ancestor is itself. In which case, to the extent that the sea is a metaphysical space and a mythic space, humans too are this sort of being. As the symbol of the 'horizon/sea-horizon' implies, the horizon of the human, which is open to the environment but at the same time closes in upon itself, is the same as the sea's horizon, within which is a space of developing paradox that is changing and yet the same, a unity of difference. Each person is a sea unto themself. And because the sea is a mythological space, the self is the hero of a myth where the interior surplus of possibility forms a multi-layered depth.

Bio-Measures Power:
Standing Before the Final Judgement of
Disease-Control=War/Politics

Yoon In-ro[1]

§1. Amidst the horror · politics · power · government, in a word, the 'political forces' following on the random rampage and infestation of the 'pestilence,' Corona[COVID-19][Coronavirus disease 2019], what procedure · method · attitude is required for thinking, with the 'audacity (daring) to know[sapere aude],' the process of governmentalizing disease(-control), which is being lain as the foundation stone in the final judgement (the last instance) of the political. The *logos*[logic/word] of the politico-economic sovereign powers facing the invisible enemy of the pandemic—for instance "I'm a wartime president"[USA, Mar 3 2020], "We are at war"[France, Mar 16 2020], "Every citizen is a commanding

---

officer of disease-control"[South Korea Apr 14 2020], "Semi-wartime situation"[China, South Korea, Italy, Spain, etc. (incl. World Health Organization)], "Victory in the people's war against coronavirus"[China], "War of Disease-Control"[Taiwan], "The battle with Corona is a marathon"[Singapore], "Victory in the Corona War"[Vietnam], "The greatest challenge[synonym: battle] since World War II"[Germany], "Border Closure · Emergency Security Measures"[UK, Denmark], "State of Emergency · Special Measures"[Japan], "Emergency Law · Emergency Measures"[Hungary] combined and calibrated in accordance with the "emergency economic situation," "wartime economic system," "special economic prescription," "economic disease-control," the emergency-Holy Binary of the political and economic, in other words the enactment of "Corona Full Mobilization"[Japan, South Korea], the declaration of "Total War on Corona"[South Korea, Japan]—in order to critique this *logos*, to begin to critique the *nomos*[law(jurisprudence)] of subjugation established · manifested by this *logos*'s efficacy · effect which is achieved through enforcement measures, to begin in the sense that 'starting is half the battle,' I find myself here and now citing from another *logos/nomos*: "the role of political power is perpetually to use a sort of silent war to reinscribe that relationship of force, and to reinscribe it in institutions, economic inequalities, language, and even the bodies of individuals. This is the initial meaning of our inversion of

Clausewitz's aphorism—politics is the continuation of war
by other means."[2]

> 1-1 Disease-control (*bang-yeok*): a war/politics
> enacted by the state, as pandemic preventer ·
> delayer[Aufhalter], to protect the lives and safety
> of its citizens. However, this pandemic is an
> exception or outlier to so-called (theory of)
> biopower (an exception in that it explains the
> totality, an outlier in that it illuminates the limits).
> For late 18th century biopower—which used
> 'statistical measures' to examine the population
> (affected by endemic disease) and thereby
> adjust and manage the effect of continuous
> death and disease in the form of statistical
> values or proportions—the 'un-known' resulting
> from inability to measure (or impossibility of
> measurement), and the (diseased) population
> increase which brought on the unpredictable
> black death, revealed its own dark limits. But
> here in 2020, biopower at its limits is enacted
> through the authority of emergency measures

---

2   Michel Foucault, *Society Must Be Defended: Lectures at the College
    de France 1975-76*, trans. David Macey, (New York: Picador,
    2003), 16.

under full-mobilization · total-war, which recode
its basic knowledge · management · control
over population and life through exclusive
right to wage war on the hidden, dormant
contagion=enemy and through (the knowledge/
light of) civil-war power which establishes
the absolute hostility of the internal, hidden
enemy=virus. Today this is a governmentalization
process as politics/war rooted in "[the expansion
of medicine], the development of medicine, the
general medicalization of behavior, modes of
conduct, discourses, desires, and so on," and the
extreme manifestation of "a sovereignty whose
luster and vigor were [...] guaranteed by [...]
medico-normalizing techniques;"[3] therefore,
the regulative complex of inter-referencing and
agreement between disciplinary and sovereign
power is adjusted, transferred, and merged by
the managerial techniques of medical science
and treatment used on the (diseased) population,
and by administrative command and measures-
taking power as disease-control=war/politics. The

---

3   Foucault, *Society Must Be Defended*, 39, 81. [The phrase "the
    expansion of medicine" is included in the Korean translation but not
    in the English — Translator's note.]

knowledges and mechanisms of normalization established complementarily within this situation: the decisive example being the "medical police," the "the management and the policing that ensure the [quiet] hygiene of an orderly society." In other words "a medicine whose main function will now be public hygiene," "which also takes the form of campaigns to teach hygiene and to medicalize the population," "with institutions to coordinate medical care, centralize power[information], and normalize knowledge."[4] The measures taken for

---

4   Foucault, *Society Must Be Defended*, 83, 244. [words in brackets are differences between the Korean and English translations — Translator's note]. The violent character of the 'medical police' can also be described with the following quotation: "The police, without the slightest relation to legal ends, not only regulate the citizen's life through self-decreed ordinances [discretionary enactment of laws] and [through discretionary enforcement] encumber him with supervision like some brute, but also in countless cases where no clear legal situation exists, 'for security reasons,' burrow into the inner workings of his life." (Walter Benjamin, "Pongryeok Bipan eul Wihayeo"[1921], in *Benyamin Seonjip 5*, trans. Choe Seong-man, (Seoul: Gil, 2008), 96. [information in brackets revises the translation via comparison with the original German (*Gesammelte Schriften*, 1991).]) [The English translator has consulted Jephcott's translation but modified it significantly to match the Korean. (Walter Benjamin, "Critique of Violence," trans. Edmond Jephcott, *Walter Benjamin: Selected Writings*, vol. 1, ed. Michael Jennings,

the safety of life are exactly this 'quiet hygiene,' 'quiet war.' Like the soviet transformation of hostilities in which revolutionary class struggle targeted with free discretion the abnormal (the sick · the deviant · the madman) for treatment and supervision to return them to an arbitrary normalcy, the 'medical police' indicates an organization that functions as a civil-war/politics to permanently extend the Soviet-like revolution/ war. The medical police is a safety mechanism for protecting society, which takes its purpose and source to be the administrative techniques of medical knowledge, which came to function as the determining factor in managing population phenomena in the late 17th century, and the light of governmental rationality which is rooted there. As a form of government contemporaneous with

---

(Cambridge: Belknap, 1996), 243.) — Translator's note]. So-called 'police authority (*Polizeigewalt* [often translated in English as 'police violence or force' — Translator's note]),' or to put it another way, the 'policing sovereign.' The basis of its legitimacy, its reason for being, the Reason of police sovereignty and cause for *gewalt* is 'for security reasons (*der Sicherheit wegen* [in the name of security]).' Under this name, before this nomenclature, under this free-discretionary right to enforce the public peace, stands the arbitrarily disregarded 'citizen's life,' 'the people's life.'

the Soviet transformation of hostility, the Nazi
state established its purpose and source in the
protection of "a society that is [...] biologically
monist"—"monistic, Statist, and biological," of
"integrity, [...] superiority, and [...] purity"—by
creating a variation on "the idea that foreigners
have infiltrated this society [which is viewed as a
biological organism], the theme of deviants who
are this [sick · polluted] society's by products."[5]
In a word, the luster and vigor of biopower which
jointly lead a Soviet/Nazi-like establishing of 'the
enemy' via the free-discretionary regulation and
application of medical-normative knowledge.
Within the synthesis of totalitarian technique and
war/politics of 'purification,' standing before the
word · law of emergency 'total mobilization*Totale
Mobilmachung* [Jünger, 1931]' and 'total war*Totale
Krieg* [The Total War, Ludendorff, 1935]' taking place
not-elsewhere-but-here, under consent to the
life-saving measures · proclamations*kerygma*,
within the economy of rescue belonging to
the measures-taking power against Corona ·
pandemic, "we all have some element of fascism

5   Foucault, *Society Must be Defended*, 80-81.

inside our heads."[6] The subject(s) constructed
amidst the political forces of the coronavirus,
and the pride and confidence towards the nation
built in the same manner. Amidst this national
feeling—both the product and motivation of
the process of subjectification through empathy
with the state—within the fiery effect of that soft
subjugation, the civil-war/measures of disease-
control · purification are reproduced as the
milestone · recovery-vehicle of consent which
leads and guides the vector of the political, and
as the agreed-upon touchstone · yardstick which
measures and discerns the purity of that vector.

1-2. Upon the absolute legitimacy-basis of
the lives of the citizens and the well-being of
society, upon the foundation of that agreement
and consensus, disease-control=war/politics is
calibrated. It makes 'creative' reference to and
exceeds the management · necessity · principle
of biopower. The reason that 'to make live'
requires a mechanism of continuous regulation
· correction · conducting · guidance, the reason
for biopower's "taking full responsibility for

6   Foucault, *Society Must Be Defended*, 30.

life," in a word, biopower's reason for governing (governmental reason/rationality), converges on none other than "distributing the living in the domain of value and utility," and in the process brings forth the following tendency, which coincides with "a phase of juridicial regression," and is then put into practice, renewed, and optimized: "that the law operates more and more as a norm, and that the judicial institution is increasingly incorporated into a continuum of apparatuses (medical, administrative, and so on) whose functions are for the most part regulatory."[7] Medicine and administration, the regulatory apparatuses which construct biopower, in a word, medicine's professional prescription · authority inter-referenced and continuously synthesized with adminstration · executive order. The glory and vigor of sovereignty rooted in this medicine≡administration, the vigor of its glory[Here the approval rating of the sovereign representative is 64 percent, May 1, 2020 (A May Day on which public assembly is prohibited · blocked).], the transfer of the citizenry's

---

7   Michel Foucault, *The History of Sexuality Volume 1: An Introduction,* trans. Robert Hurley, (New York: Pantheon Books, 1978), 144.

legislative power decided by its correlation
· subordination to this regulatory executive
power[Here the birth of the 180-seat massive ruling party, April
16, 2020 (The sixth anniversary of the 'April 16 Sewolho' disaster,
with one year left on the statute of limitations)],the weakening
· reversal of the trend toward the "judicialization
of politics." This 'regression of the legislative
and judicial' is another way of describing the
circumstances of government under which the
juridicial is indicated · guided · transformed ·
recoded by the discretionary enforcement of
measures-taking power, which is absolutized
by the responsibility of protecting life. To put
it another way, the administration=measures-
taking-power which, after seizing the monopoly
on prevention and right of first occupancy in
decisions about the state of emergency · urgency
regarding living · life at the level of the personal
and the totality at one and the same time, cuts in
front of the judicial and legislative—one might
call them the political forms of 'chatter'—and
leads with them following after-the-fact · in-
retinue. Or to put it yet another way, the measures-
taking power which is rooted in the promise ·
guarantee and right · obligation to protect life
and society, the administrative-measures led

by the presently ongoing and future · potential
procurement and enforcement of legitimacy, the
administrative rationality which measures · tests
· extracts · produces the reproducibility of its
own optimized and revitalized forces along the
measures-taking vector of power relations that
places the safety of life at center. Here the specific
distribution of these force relations functions
as the last instance of disease-control=war/
politics, and as the source and purpose of
measures-taking power which resembles a war-
of-prevention for the sake of 'life.' Amidst the
political circumstances of Corona, amidst the
specific force relations under which biopower
can be named bio-measures power[Bio-Maßnahme
macht], bio-power[bio-pouvoir] constructs · percusses
· examines · establishes the laboratory · limits ·
frontline · points-of-contact for its own optimized
and revitalized manifestation. In a word, this is the
shift from biopower to bio-measures power.

1-2-a. The force of this 'measures-taking'—
'*mutatis mutandis*[discretionary changes · modifications
to law]' as so-called 'violence'—in other words,
the free-discretionary interpretation of the law
and execution of authority, indicates that the

governance of life that takes both its source and method to be (preventative · emergency · special) measures^{Maßnahme} is an authority rooted in none other than arbitrary and discretionary proclamation · establishment · manufacturing · synthesis with regard to legal exceptions^{Ausnahme}, namely the suspension of the law and the expansion of what resides within/without the borders of the law. The Hobbesian question of 'who interprets' and 'who decides' is presided-over · monopolized · led within the political forces of Corona by disease-control's right of war, the right to take measures regarding life. As an example of this sort of legal exception, the "Law Regarding Emergency Measures in Response to the Coronavirus Epidemic[France, Mar. 24, 2020 (translated and published on the homepage of the French Embassy in Korea on March 25, 2020)]," which is the document that concretely establishes the 'we are at war' *logos/nomos* of the wartime sovereign(s), consists of articles relevant to the 'measures' which take effect under its declaration of a "health state of emergency"—namely the "decree" of "limitations," "prohibitions," "quarantine," "closures," "restrictions," "regulations," "punishment," "imprisonment,"

and "nullification." "Exceptional" measures
undertaken promptly amidst the 'unprecedented'
spread of infection to the life and health of
the citizenry, amidst the exceptional, without
parallel, emergency of the pandemic. Or to put it
another way, government by measures, which by
discretionarily deciding a state of exception that
suspends law and government by law, achieve the
synthesis of vigor[executive power] and glory[legitimacy
· reign]. With the foundation of a "Scientific
Investigation Council"—as an accumulation ·
consultant · supervisor · regulatory-apparatus
of decisive, scientific[medical] knowledges which
guarantee the state of synthesis of bio-measures
power, this 'state of exception' of rampaging
pestilence is operated as a laboratory for the
pure implementation of unhindered government.
Through such "exceptional measures[l'exception
des mesures]"—which form the core of "economic
measures" and "social adaptation measures"—
the "distribution" of government under
normal circumstances is regulated · amended
· appropriated · reconstructed. By "exercising
the power of decree[decret (the sovereign · transcendent's
command · ordinance · volition), the regulatory capability
of this distribution manifests as emergency

administrative orders and preemptive prevention-measures, which are more fundamentally a discretionary and preventative resolution on the "necessary scope" of the exercise of that power. Or in other words, it manifests as a process of consent and subjugation for the sake of the protection of life.

1-2-b. Measures and consent, the 'situation of measures' implemented by consent, the 'situation of consent' to measures. As a text which indicates the nature of this situation, let us take Brecht's learning-play *He Who Says Yes* (we could also choose *The Measures Taken*[Both were first performed, revised, and published in magazines in 1930-1931]) and observe the ramifications of that choice. Brecht wrote *The Measures Taken* as an expansion of *He Who Says Yes* after the bloody suppression of May Day demonstrations by the ruling party (Social Democratic Party) in 1929, when he came to believe the German Communist Party to be the only group strong enough to stand up to the Nazis (National Socialist German Workers' Party). Thus, in *He Who Says Yes*, the source of the situationality of 'taking measures' is expressed, and moreover that source is specifically placed in the midst of a rampaging pestilence[on a related note, in the *The Resistable Rise of Arturo Ui* (1941), Brecht portrays Hitler as a 'pest']. The teacher, one of the play's characters, begins the plot with the following dialogue: "I shall soon be starting on a journey to the mountains. A terrible disease has broken out among us, and in the city beyond the mountains live several great doctors."[8] Following this conversation, which the teacher has with his young student's mother who has caught the infectious "disease^Seuche[contagion

---

8   Bertolt Brecht, "Ye rago Haneun Saram, Anio rago Haneun Saram," *Beurehiteu Seonjip 1*, trans. Jo Gil-ye, ed. Hanguk Beurehiteu Hakhoe, (Seoul: Yeongeuk Gwa Ingan, 2011), 440. Quotations below will not be footnoted, and revisions to the translation follow the original, B. Brecht, »Der Jasager und der Neinsager«, in: *Versuche*, Heft 4 (Separatdruck: 11-12), Berlin: Kiepenheuer, 1930. (This offprint · rebound edition consists only of three plays— *He Who Says Yes*, *He Who Says No*, and *The Measures Taken*— in their first release, materially illustrating the relationship of these three learning-plays [These linked plays also mesh with the story "Measures against Authority (*Gewalt*)," one of the *Stories of Mr. Keuner*, published in the fifth issue of the same magazine, *Experiments (Versuche).*]) [English translations follow Sauerlande's translation, modifying it in some places to match the Korean translation and revisions. Bertolt Brecht, "He Who Says Yes / He Who Says No," trans. Wolfgang Sauerlande, *The Measures Taken and Other Lehrstücke*, eds. John Willet and Ralph Manheim, (New York: Arcade, 2001). — Translator's note].

· malady]," the teacher and the boy he teaches set out with the relief expedition to get "medicine and instruction^{Unterweisung [religious(=medical) instruction · guidance]}," along with three university students. Regarding the boy setting out on the expedition, the mother and the teacher say: "Many consent to wrong things; he, however / Does note consent to illness, but holds [consents] that / Illness should be cured." Those who set out amidst the rampage of the disease to seek medical prescription and religious guidance consent^{Einverständnis [permission · agreement]} to the absolute purpose of life-saving measures, to the process of march and progress to save life and the city. But when the boy, who consented with them, falls ill in the mountains and can't go on, that consent functions as a binding power to force the boy to consent irresistibly/ voluntarily to the forfeiting of his own life, to the measure of having his body hidden at the bottom of a cliff, after being thrown into the valley. The teacher feels sorry for the boy and "asks" him whether he consents to be killed, but really that question functions as a procedure of formal justification for the already irreversible— regardless of the boy's consent—decision which safeguards the march and progress towards treatment and instruction for the sake of disease-control. In response to that question the boy, in accordance with "Custom," following the old, deeply-stacked interpretations and ceremonies of decision, says, "Yes," and the teacher proclaims, "He has answered in accordance^gemäß [agreement · conformity] with necessity^Notwendigkeit [inevitability · unavoidability]." Afraid to be left alone to die, the boy "demands" to be thrown into the valley, and the momentarily hesitating university students respond, "Yes," when the consent-seeking teacher asks them, "You have decided to go ahead and leave him behind. / It is easy to decide his fate^Schicksal / But hard to carry out the decision. / Are you ready to hurl him into the valley?" Who is this teacher, who leads the university students by asking their consent? The decider · guide to the law of necessity which even the gods dare not fight, the fuhrer [guide · commander (divine providence · manager)]. The head · Duce^[leader · conductor] who leads the march · progress to produce, this is what decides the measures-taking vector. The measures of life and death, giving and taking away, brought upon the boy who consents to his own death in agreement with the necessity of disease-control. The situationality of 'the measures taken^Die Maßnahme' is at one and the same time a management of regulatory power relations which takes^nehmen in hand the measuring-stick^maß [standard · criterion] and, without excess or deficiency, measures^messen the measured^maßen [appropriate]-amount · optimum levels, and also an economy of arbitrary, discretionary power relations which decide upon the suspension · exception of the measuring stick—a state in which measure is taken-away^maß-nehmen [In a related point, Carl Schmitt, discussing his own 'theory of measures,' once said to reference Brecht's *The Measures Taken*]. Amidst this free-discretionary enforcement rooted in the simultaneous retention and removal of the measuring stick, the boy is thrown into the valley of bitter cold and death. As the university students cover the boy's corpse with clods of earth, the chorus sings. "None guiltier than his neighbor." Who is this neighbor? Who is the 'guilty one^schuldinger [indebted one]' who initiated the enforcement relations of such measures? (i) The students who leave the student to die and bury his body? (ii) The teacher who said it was inevitable, for the sake of life amid the disease and the salvation of the city, and then led the others to consent and take these measures? (iii) The chorus

who consented to asking for the boys consent, and
who asked the question in unison? (iv) The people
of the city, who fell ill and await the bringing of
medicine and instruction? As a learning-play,
"He Who Says Yes" forces us to study the issue
of life-saving measures taken in accordance with
the constitutive political elements of disease
and consent (to such measures); of consent to
the onward march and progress which are taken
as means to the ends of disease-control, and the
measures rooted in such consent; of how to think
the network of these measures, and how the
violence of such measures becomes involved in
justice, legitimacy, and the law. The first lines sung
by the chorus in the beginning of the learning-
play, in fact, state the necessity · inevitability of
learning about this sort of consent: "What we
must learn above all is consent. / Many say yes,
and yet there is no consent. / Many are not asked,
and many / Consent to wrong things. Therefore:
/ What we must learn above all is consent." Here
the political circumstances of the pandemic, the
specific circumstances of disease-control=war/
politics were already illuminated in this learning-
play by Brecht.

§2. Alongside the viewpoint of intersection · reference · distribution, the relationship of biopower and sovereign power can also be seen from the differing viewpoint of 'excess,' and it is here that these two powers display once more a certain extreme and exceptional character. One is "atomic power" as biopower in excess of sovereign power, and the other is the excess of biopower over sovereign power that appears "when it becomes technologically and politically possible for man not only to manage life but to make it proliferate, to create living matter, to build the monster, and ultimately, to build viruses that cannot be controlled and that are universally destructive."[9] Since this regulatory government, or governmental regulation— through techno-political creation and utilization of viruses as one methodology and ontology of biopower—is one historical form and specific extreme of the biopower that has developed since the nineteenth century through experiment · conjecture · accumulation of knowledge for the sake of monopolistic possession of life, the present progressive expression of this apparatus of knowledge-power[or power-truth] is the research laboratory run by economic cooperation[division of labor] among the countries of the world. (In the context of power · responsibility relations between nations, the laboratory that has been pointed

---

9   Foucault, *Society Must Be Defended*, 253-254.

at as a possible source of the coronavirus pandemic—
Wuhan Institute of Virology, Chinese Academy of Sciences
(est. 1956)—was conducting a pathogen modification
research project ['virus variant gain-of-function study'] which had
previously been conducted in the United States before
being outsourced after the US administration ended it
with a moratorium. Behind the system of moratorium
and outsourcing lies the danger of virus variants, and the
impossibility of full control.) Biopower as a complex of
public health · military · political · industrial goals, and the
virus research laboratory as secret-apparatus. The position
and function of this apparatus—its function, in other words,
as the scientific advanced guard for prevention · detection
· disinfection · delineation · control · immunity in relation
to pathogens, and as the front line and Maginot Line, at
once, of knowledge of life generally—is to embody the
impossibility of full control over viruses[chimera viruses] tested
and created under biopower's state of excess, a particular
situation in which a techno-politics of universal destruction
is made manifest. The spectroscope that reveals this extremity
is the rampaging pestilence, the case-of-emergency · political-
array of the pandemic. Here biopower, in the form of a
bio-measures power which resynthesizes · recodes the
right to take measures, functions as the distributor of
disease-control=war/politics. It is a process of standing
up to this 'greatest challenge' by proclaiming biopower's

law-silencing wartime state, a process of redistributing ·
resetting the relationship with sovereign principles and
methods, and biopower will be driven to an existential
crossroads depending on its success in overcoming this
challenge. Thus, here in the case-of-emergency of the
pandemic, biopower stands before its own testing pad
and launchpad, atop what is at once a steppingstone and
stumbling stone. As the pandemic has dropped the curtain
on that biopower which has been around since the French
Revolution of the eighteenth century, it was recognized
as an irresistible, random, temporary drama of death, but
here the political array of the pandemic ultimately, as a
force that demanded a change in the distribution of power
relations, is deciding the vector, technology, tendency,
intensity, speed of measures-taking war/politics and the
state of world-political leadership. Today the exceptional
drama of disease and disease-control—as ultimately
neither temporary nor unending, and as something spread
· strengthened · enforced by the size · strength · effect of
class · racial · regional difference, in the form of a final
judgement in a dormant · potential war/politics, repeatedly
experimenting with the possibility of administration and
resistance—takes on the character, when the curtain goes
up, of a sort of measures-play[Maßnahme-spiel]. The present
case-of-emergency · political-array performed in this play
· theater leads to a redistribution of governance relations,

as the accelerator · determinant · guiding force bringing on
a recoding for the sake of biopower's creative self-renewal
and transformation, and as a solvent melting away the
political in general, previously formulated as a procurement
technique of the authenticity · legitimacy · legality · suitability
of government, and as the technique of subjugation and
formation of a national feeling. Here the pandemic's case-
of-emergency is a sort of end of biopower's history of
development towards monopolistic possession of life, its
decisive theatrical staging and edition, and this point of
ending · demise is the hotspot · apex at which all the self-
experimental tangent lines of biopower pass.

2-1. In this excess · end · hotspot of biopower,
one possible outlook for another vector of
power reaching toward possession of life is
the synthesis of a foundation of disciplinary
information technology under the name of so-
called 'K-Quarantine (*K-Bang-yeok*; K-disease-control).'
For example, the Ministry of the Interior and
Safety's Self-Quarantine Safety Protection app,
the Corona notifications app which publishes
contact tracing information on confirmed cases,
the Corona map app that displays the distribution
of confirmed cases, along with CCTV, the
display of information about confirmed cases in

the media and SNS, the inquiry and collection of computerized personal medical records and credit card purchase histories, and so on—all of which form a network of administration · medical facilities · telecom companies · credit card companies · police measures interlinked with digitalized archives of information about daily life and consumption. And then the formation of consent to administrative decrees directly securing and making these measures mandatory. The spread of consent to such measures is misperceived and defended as a mature, enlightened, advanced democratic political system. That is, measures-taking democratic government. The society that must be protected in this contradictory state of planing-off is always controlled by the proper category of the perpetually administered society. Here measures-taking democratic government manifests in laws like the following: "In order to prevent infectious diseases, the Minister of Health and Welfare, Mayors/Do[Province] Governors, or heads of Sis/Guns/Gus[cities/counties/ districts] shall take all or some of the following measures"[Infectious Disease Control and Prevention Act, Chapter 8 Preventative Measures, Article 49, National Law Information Center, Korea]. In other words, it is a chain

of discretionary measures-taking declared by
administrative representatives at each stage · unit
· scale · level of administration. As an example
of the digital-mobile probationary technology
used under the broad consent to this process, we
can take the real-time integration · networking ·
utilization of information[Ubiquitous Sensor Network]
built on location tracking devices attached to the
body (body-integrated) with Radio Frequency
Identification[RFID] tags · labels · cards · chips. At
one extreme of digital-mobile surveillance devices
related to the body is surveillance technology
integrated with the body, already in common use
in the form of vaccine-microchip technology
used for insertion into the bodies of companion
animals. Vaccines used to achieve herd immunity,
as one form of disease-control measures, function
as the foundation stone to consensus and consent
to the legitimacy-basis for such technologies
of government. At that point, the safety of
life becomes the transparent veil-ideology of
governance, and safety measures taken for the
sake of life become the final-judgement=black-
hole of the political. In this way, the apparatus
of voluntary subjugation is put back in motion,
and the individual is constructed · produced as a

channel—a catalyst · medium—of power. Thus, again, fascism is in all of our heads: "In actual fact, one of the first effects of power is that it allows bodies, gestures, discourses and desires to be identified and constituted as something individual. The individual is not, in other words, power's opposite number; the individual is one of power's first effects. The individual is in fact a power-effect, and at the same time, and to the extent that he is a power effect, the individual is a relay: power passes through the individuals it has constituted. [...] I say, 'Power is exercised, circulates, and forms networks,' We can also say 'We all have some element of fascism inside our heads,' or at a more basic level still, 'We all have some element of power in our bodies.'"[10] The subjugation effect at the level of individuation constructed by this power, and the experiment of limitless governmental · regulatory acceleration at the level of the total population via catalyzation · mediation, are attempted by excess/virtual biopower rooted in conversion to the digital · mobile · archival in the midst of the emergency of the pandemic here and now, and by nanny-

---

10   Foucault, *Society Must Be Defended*, 29-30.

state[Iain Macleod, 1965] biopower redistributed ·
rearmed in the manner of bio-measures power.
This place—this point · hotspot or frontline
· Maginot line—is where the process of
governmentalization is tested in the form of civil
war as the regulatory continuation · speed-shifts
of disease-control=war/politics, and in the form
of the interpretations and decisions of civil-war
management. These interpretations and decisions
are complementary to capitalistic accumulation
and investment, and in fact are decidedly led—
designed · coded—by capital accumulation: "This
bio-power was without question an indispensable
element in the development of capitalism; the
latter would not have been possible without
the controlled insertion of bodies into the
machinery of production and the adjustment of the
phenomena of population to economic processes.
But this was not all it required; it also needed the
growth of both these factors, their reinforcement
as well as their availability and docility; it had
to have methods of power capable of optimizing
forces, aptitudes, and life in general without at the
same time making them more difficult to govern."
The "investment of the body, its valorization,

and the distributive management of its forces"[11]
necessary to this is here achieved through urgent
(special · preventative) measures, under the name
of a bureaucratic "economic normalization[Term
used outside South Korea, Apr 20 2020]," or as a war/politics
of normalizing the abnormal through "economic
disease-control[Term used within South Korea, Apr 20
2020]." The plague that has infected the economy,
in a word, the public vector (the regulations on
private profit for the sake of public management)
that pollutes · infects the free and natural cycle of
the economy. Amidst the guillotine measures of
economic disease-control which puts this vector's
head on the block, the "Korean New Deal" and
"digitalized · contact-free economy[South Korea, May
7 2020]" become repetitive, comedic-sanguinary
mottos supporting the myth (deification) of
profit.[12] The tangent lines of economic measures

11 Foucault, *History of Sexuality,* 140-141.
12 As hastily revealed by the amendments to the 'Three Data
    Economy Bills (Personal Information Act · Data Network Act ·
    Credit Information Act)' proposed in November 2018 and passed
    on January 9, 2020, the amendment process was ratified · justified
    · reinforced · accelerated after-the-fact by the political situation of
    the pandemic here and now, where 'economic disease-control' plays
    the bass note to economic policy. Information on sexual · medical

and profit pass tenaciously close at this point of excess, the limit-point · hotspot, of biopower. The self-experiments of biopower, or the measures of disease-control=war/politics, pass bad-infinitely at the sacred vertex of profit. The individuals constructed as the intermediary · medium of politico-economic power within this devilish-double complementarity · interconditionality of measures; and the totality · society which can

---

· health conditions such as psychiatric · urological · gynecological illness histories and treatment records, information regarding ideology and belief status such as registration and withdrawal from unions · political parties, information on individual financial · credit conditions and so on, as the primary data necessary to digitalized · contact-free economy, became legally utilizable under "exceptional" and "special case" provisions decided "by presidential decree." These uses are expressed in the amendment with the legal term "processing": "The term 'processing' means the collection, generation, connecting, interlocking, recording, storage, retention, value-added processing, editing, searching, output, correction, recovery, use, provision, disclosure, and destruction of personal information and other similar activities" (Personal Information Protection Act – Partial Amendment, Feb 4 2020). This was enforced after further adjustment of detailed provisions by ordinance of the Ministry of Public Administration and Security (Apr 1 2020). This partial amendment is not simply a single law of a single nation, but was based on and legislated in conjunction with the 'EU General Data Protection Regulation (GDPR)' enacted in May of 2018.

only be constructed through these individuated individuals and can only in that way be protected. In a word, the safety-measurificaton society, life-saving totalitarianism. It is reproduced here within the political forces of the pandemic in the form of life-recognizing · conquering violence and the specific conditions of societal distribution · monopoly achieved through this violence.

2-2. The problem framed and the solution suggested in the name "economic disease-control"—that is, a planned-economy/economic-planning enacted by measures-taking-administration/administrative-measures— is carried out as a disease-control/war which defines the enemy=contagion as the regulations · recession · contradictions · terror that attack and pollute the capitalist economy and bring about its stoppage and end, or in other words, as acts of terror against the secure territory of the economy. Under the motto of economic disease-control, disease-control measures are already not limited to the realm of administrative authority against infectious diseases, but instead perceive the conditions of the economy as a crisis situation similar to war-time and expand

into the active realm of thinking up effective
responses. In accordance with the infection ·
spread of the pandemic, and using that terror as a
stepping stone, disease-control measures become
generalized · rampant as anything 'relating to
disease-control,' an issue of war/politics. It is
as if the terms necessary to compose the phrase
disease-control=war/politics were already capable
of compatibility · transference · synthesis. Just as,
in the midst of terror over the contagion, the name
'wuhan virus' immediately came to signify asian
race, and was viewed with hostility, hatred, and
scorn in a sort of yellow peril; just as, in the midst
of the surpassing of sovereign power by biopower,
a politics of terror under the name of terror(ism)
keeps pace with the process of manufacturing
uncontrollable viruses; just as disease-control
against the virus Seuchenbekämpfung[disease control]
and the war on terror Bekämpfung des Terrorismus
construct inter-compatible and synthesizable
micro-politico-biologies of fear and invasion.
This is the creativity · reproductive power of
the expansive switching of places, and self-
displacement, of pandemic=war/politics,
which interprets and establishes the politico-
economic infection=enemy with free discretion,

which devises and extracts technologies of management against the virus=enemy under the state of emergency. Let us resolve to restart in a different way by examining one old but contemporary representation related to this equation of contagion=enemy, and to measures of governmentalization=subjugation similar to those of disease-control=war/politics. This new beginning is rooted in the following statement: "Governmentalization [...] cannot apparently be dissociated from the question 'how not to be governed?'"[13]

§3. *Politike Techne*—the techniques of 'managing' the *polis*, or the political · community—what is called in *Protagoras* "art of politics," "governance techniques to lead the state," "techniques for managing the country," "civic techniques;" and that which is distributed and functions as a directly related part of this: "techniques of war[polemike]," "art of politics."[14] Protagoras tells the story of humankind,

---

13 Michel Foucault, *The Politics of Truth*, trans. Lysa Hocroth and Catherine Porter, (Los Angeles: Semiotext(e), 2007), 44.

14 Plato, *Protagoras*, 322b. The various translations quoted here are taken from the following versions. (Bak Hong-gyu, "*Peurotagoraseu* e Daehan Bunseok," *Huirap Cheolhak Nongo*, (Seoul: Mineumsa, 1995), 79; Peullaton, "*Peurotagoraseu*,"

who were unable to possess these techniques because of
Epimetheus' initial insufficient/incorrect distribution of
skills, and who then dissipated into a condition of scattered
groups · crowds[a multitude (multitudo)] and were mercilessly
slaughtered by wild beasts. When they gathered in order
to avoid this, their lack of such techniques led the humans
to act unjustly towards each other, and this was a sort of
orderlessness, anomie—where the strong eat the weak
and there is violence between humans, where the mass of
people is no more than wolves to each other, a zero-state of
respect and deference towards others, an unethical · unjust
state of disorder—and as a result, humankind "scattered
here and there once again and were perishing[scattered once
more and started to be slaughtered again; again scattered and then were killed;

Peullaton Jeonjip 3, trans. Cheon Byeong-hui, (Seoul: Sup, 2019),
222; Peullaton, "Peurotagoraseu," *Peurotagoraseu · Lakeseu ·
Menon*, trans. Bak Jong-hyeon, (Paju: Seogwangsa, 2010), 81;
Peullaton, *Peurotagoraseu*, trans. Gang Seong-hun, (Seoul: EJ
Books, 2012), 55.) Closely related to "good advice to help one
properly manage one's household" (318e), the art-of-management
of the *polis* is the manifestation of '*politike sophia*,' meaning "wise
polis management" (321d) and consists of making the people of the
polis live in '*politike arete*,' or "civic virtue" (324a). [The English
translation follows the original Korean translations in this section in
order to render the noted translation differences, but the translator
has consulted, Plato, "Protagoras," *Plato in Twelve Volumes*, vol. 3,
trans. W.R.M. Lamb, (Cambridge: Harvard University Press, 1967).
— Translator's note]

again scattered and fell into decline]." Seeing this, "Zeus, fearing
that our human race would go completely extinct, sent
Hermes to the humans to bring them a sense of shame[awe ·
respect (aidōs); shame] and justice[dikē], so that shame and justice
would become the principles, in constructing communities
and forming bonds of friendship[allowing order among the countries
and ties of friendship binding each to the other to arise; to make the city orderly
and merge the people; by which order of the country and unity of the people
could gather them together]."[15] After telling Hermes to divvy out
justice and a sense of shame to everyone rather than only to
a few people like the other skills, Zeus explains, "If justice
and a sense of shame belong only to a minority, a nation
will not be able to arise[will be unable to form]" and then orders:
"let anyone who cannot be given a sense of shame and
justice be considered a **pestilence upon the community**[a
plague upon the city; a sickness of the country; an affliction of the country] and
be killed and removed[be put to death; be punished; be killed], and
put forth[establish] a law in my name to decree this."[16] Life/
death decided by Zeus, a disease-control-like law of life
and death, giving and taking away. The lack of shame; the
injustice of the one considered a pestilence; the diseased

---

15 Plato, *Protagoras*, 322c. The translation is a synthesis of the
    versions cited above.
16 Plato, *Protagoras*, 322c-d. The translation is a synthesis of the
    versions cited above. The emphasis is the author's. From here
    citations to this source will be in-text.

as the enemy of the *polis*. The punishment of that enemy, which is known as disease-control=war. This is the art-of-politics that brings order to people living together, and it is at once the basis which constitutes the management · governmental techniques of the *polis* and the transposition/avant-garde[17] form of the art of war which functions as a directly related part of that governmental technique. The law of disease-control=war/politics established and enforced in the name of Zeus, the law of final-judgement measures by Zeus who decides life · death · giving · taking-away, and the human life · living that lives or dies before that law.

> 3-1. Zeus's foundation of national law as disease-control regarding the diseased as enemy, and the *gewalt* of life-saving death penalty allotment · regulation · guidance. Standing 'before the law' of Zeus signed · stamped by the dispatched Hermes is the legitimacy-basis of law enforcement that turns the enactment of this national law—as the establishment · preservation of the absent Zeus's regent presence—into an expansion of the place of 'justice.' This is the "plague of the *polis*νόσον πόλεως,"[*Platonis Opera*, Vol. 3, 322d5, ed. Johannes Burnet, 1905]—or pestilence upon the community—

---

17   [These are homophones in Korean. — Translator's note]

that constitutes wartime · state-of-emergency, and it is disease-control against the invading · rampant 'diseased.' The word for 'plague,' *nósos*, means 'contagious disease · illness' and by extension 'sickness · unwholesomeness · debauchery · catastrophe (caused by god or nature) · disaster. The plague · *nósos* spreading through the state, staining the state, refers to the pollution of life gathered within the state, the life of debauchery and indulgence sickening the state, the enemy of the state that orders invasion of the state by unstoppable catastrophe. The art-of-politics as disease-control/war against the diseased, or state management as disease-control · measures-taking art-of-government, establishes as its purpose and source the "techniques of measurement(metrētikē)" as the "means of saving life."(356d) This knowledge of measurement is related to the selection of strength · speed · size · distance · elevation · thickness · amount · function · visibility · hiddenness · beauty · ugliness · harmony · joy · pain. On this basis, Socrates offers the following questions and answers: "What is it that can save our life(bios)? Is it not knowledge(epistēmē)? Is it not a kind of art of measurement? Since this is the technique relating

to excess(hyperbolē) and insufficiency."(357a) Life(or
bios as living · life (only))-saving knowledge, the
art of measurement—in other words, knowledge
via the techniques of measurement, or the art of
measurement concerning knowledge which acts as
a guide in establishing and preserving the optimum
level regulated to avoid excess and insufficiency
in a given situation. The metaphor used to
simultaneously capture this art-of-measurement/
art-of-government and knowledge, which are
rooted in each other, is the "steersman"(344d)
and his "command of the ship,"(344c) and the
knowledge of "study on the treatment[care
(therapeia)] of patients" which makes the "excellent
doctor."(345a) Amidst "a kind of prediction[foresight
· expectation] of something bad,"[358c] the
measurement necessary in guiding the ship to
avoid the storm before meeting it; the necessity
of the knowledge · measurement of prescription
and diagnosis to maintain health and avoid
death and disease. The knowledge · technique
· interpretation · decision · power · authority
of steersman and doctors learned · cultivated ·
procured · prepared · executed by that necessity,
for that necessity—this is the sign of state
management's art-of-government. Conversely, not

the command of the ship but the wreck · distress
of the ship and the mutiny · commandeering of
the ship by pirates or the enslaved; not the care
of life but the decline · necrosis of life and the
confusion · imbalance of the body and the soul,
and so on, are because of "insufficient art of
measurement,"[357d] the doctor and the steersman's
"ignorance.[amathia]"[358c] Or because of the
indecision lying in ambush within the ignorance
of the doctor and steersman. Because of the
recklessness of wandering and confused steering ·
treatment. The diseased, that which is considered
a plague upon the polis, infiltrates the knowledge
· art-of-government that is measurement, in
relation to the state as doctor · steersman, with
the state of confusion · disharmony · excess-and-
insufficiency · recklessness. This is the reason
that the poets are expelled. Poets are "those
whose only work is fractious conversation about
things which they cannot prove,"[347b] and this is
indecisive idle chatter, the disposal of predictions,
where steering and diagnosis have fallen into self-
indulgence. "Putting the poets aside, we must use
our own strength to make discussion amongst
ourselves. Testing ourselves, and the truth."[348a]
The unnecessity of the poets, the "expulsion or

exclusion"342c of the poets. In a word, the law of
Zeus which expels the diseased poets · enemies,
the culling law of disease-control.

3-2 Protagoras, inheritor of the law of Zeus carried
out against the plague=enemy of the polis, speaks:
"If there is, in fact, a single thing in which all
citizens must be involved in order for there to be
a country,[for a state · community to be erected and preserved]
what could it be? [...] If that one thing is not the
carpenter's technique or the blacksmith's or the
potter's technique, but rather justice[rightness] and
restraint[a wholesome mind (sōphrosynē)] and reverence—
in short what can be called, linking all three
together, 'human excellence[aretē]'— [...] then
those who cannot share in it, whether they be child
or man or woman, will be taught and punished,
and will be so until they have been made better,
and whoever fails to conform despite punishment
and teaching must, as an incurable person, be
expelled from their countries or executed."(324e-
325b) The justice · restraint · reverence which
construct human excellence. First, 'restraint.' As
a technique related to the overall balance of the
phalanx of individual hoplites facing the enemy,
it is the condition which maintains pace and

regulates the harmony of the whole, and a form of
morality(virtue) · knowledge of the cooperative
art-of-war which engenders that condition. As
a form of control over the integral · organic
relations · order that constitutes the individual
and the whole, it draws out · derives the optimum
state of power with which to face the enemy. As
this technique of restraint is the primary form of
the art-of-war/art-of-politics which looks after
the *polis-like bios*—the specific distribution
of the unified assembly—and it's livelihood,
it is only within this condition of restraint that
the law of Zeus—its legitimacy found in the
livelihood · caretaking · inclusion of *bios* and the
legal violence of killing · expelling · excluding
the *bios*—can be established and defended as
permanent 'justice.' In this way, the justice of the
law of Zeus—which places life's livelihood and
extinguishing at the center of its enactment—
is a type of *gewalt* which uses the technique
· knowledge of restraint in relation to life as
a means to regulate and reset the relations of
legitimacy and legality in the manner appropriate
to a given situation. The divine nature of these
appropriate bounds of government, the regulatory
line which divides what is within the law from

what is without. The motivation for and product of knowing, following, exalting this absolute line/ good[18] in a type of subjugation/subjectification is 'reverence.' Within this synthesis of restraint · justice · reverence, in other words, within human excellence · *aretē*, individuals function as the medium · intermediary of the whole by voluntarily discussing and becoming involved in the persistence of the state, and in doing so have the livelihood of the *bios* conferred upon them. Since "in order for there to be a state [...] everyone must enthusiastically talk to and teach each other, without hoarding or hiding, about the proper[right · just [ta dikia] and the lawful[ta nomina],"(327a-b) the greatest effect delivered by these simultaneously individual-and-total, total-and-individual relations, and the greatest efficacy of balancing the art-of-treatment and art-of-steering, is that they "produce health and good bodily conditions, the preservation of countries, domination over others, and wealth."(354b)

3-3. The diagnosis and prescription against the rampage of the plague-like enemy; the steering

---

18 [These are homophones in Korean. — Translator's note]

and command of the ship infested by that enemy.
The process of the art-of-government which
is always recovering the appropriate bounds
within which restraint, justice, and reverence
can operate, is also a process of correcting
the injustice · irreverence rampant within the
condition of unrestraint, in other words the
condition of arrogance · hubris[hybris] or indulgence
· recklessness. The art-of-measurement/art-of-
government of the doctor and the steersman
is soon constructed as a corrective technique
complementary to death-penalty · execution
and simultaneous with the law of expulsion ·
exclusion, a technique of setting-straight, "so
that one cannot act just however one wills."
"This is just the same as when those who teach
letters[(grammatistēs)] first draw the letters in faintly
with the pen for their unskilled pupils, and then
give them the copy-book and have them write by
following their outlines. Just so the city sketches
the [faintly traced] outlines of the laws[nomoi],
and since these are the designs of excellent
lawmakers of the past, demands that they govern
and be governed by these laws, and punishes
those who deviate from them. The name for
this punishing[punishment], since in many places

punishment through trial is disciplinary, can be called discipline[correction(euthynai)]."(326d) The correction · ordering of indulgence · disorder which does not follow the guidance of the laws and 'acts however it wills.' If one does not follow voluntarily and enthusiastically, and threatens to make indulgence rampant, "they are set straight with threats and lashes, as one would straighten a twisted and bent piece of wood."(325d) This art-of-correction/art-of-government is depicted as a process of children—none other than children are taken as the first citizens/subjects of the state's establishment—being guided along the dotted line of the law, thus packing and filling in the dotted line of the law to be a continuous line, and enacting it. The law which doles out lashings for the sake of this enactment, the children who are the medium[19] of the law. Within this discipline, this mother · father · nanny's concern for looking-after · taking-care of the children; within the "right conduct[eukosmia (good behavior)] of the children"(325e) raised and cultured this way, the voluntary subjugation of the 'the proper and the lawful' is

---

19 [Here the Korean words for 'lashing' and 'medium' are homophones. — Translator's note]

always being carried out. The caretaking process of government acts on none other than the "souls of children," so "that they may become more gentle more graceful, and more harmonious, and thereby more useful in speech and action."(326b) The art-of-measure that says soul≡truth; in a word, the knowledge · technique which maintains the optimal condition of state management by synthesizing soul and truth. This is the *bios*' means of saving life, the foundation and limit of the disease-control-like art-of-politics/art-of-war upon the infestation of the plague-like enemy: "The art of measurement, by revealing the truth(to alēthes), brings the soul in to rest within the truth and maintain tranquility, and thereby saves life."(356e)

§4. The *bios* saved by the conjoining process of soul and truth. In other words, the internal life · living of the polis that is saved within the process of derivation and maintenance for the joining of soul≡truth; the life · living that becomes internalized through this process · litigation, standing before the jurisprudence of the *polis*. The soul≡life established as the original object of government while the art-of-measurement—as knowledge · technique for the justice and legality of state management—structures the restrained/absolute distribution of individual and

whole. The following two passages problematize this
process by considering i) the character of critique, which
inserts a second opinion on the truth when it is engaged in
observation · pharmacology · prescription and is discovered
· concealed · proclaimed by the law of Zeus or the platonic
steersman · doctor's art-of-measurement, and ii) a care-
taking of the soul which differs from that of the doctor ·
steersman's art-of-measurement, and the character of a
counter-knowledge · technique which would make such
care-taking possible.

> i) And if governmentalization(gouvernementali
> sation) is indeed this movement through which
> individuals are subjugated in the reality of a
> social practice through mechanisms of power that
> adhere to a truth, well, then! I will say that critique
> is the movement by which the subject gives
> himself the right to question truth on its effects of
> power and [the right to] question power on [the]
> discourses of truth [produced by that power].
> Well, then!: critique will be the art of voluntary
> insubordination, that of reflected intractability.
> Critique would essentially ensure the desubjugatio
> n(désassujettissement) of the subject in the context
> of what we could call, in a word, the politics of

truth.[20]

ii) [Think of] All the metaphors of parrēsia as assuring the therapeuein(care-taking) of the soul; it is an art similar to the art of medicine [treatment], to the art of piloting [steering], and similar also to the art of government and political action. Spiritual direction, piloting [steering], medicine [treatment], the art of politics, the art of the kairos.[21]

Governmentalization=subjugation as the object of critique=desubjugation. Daring to speak truth[boldness · courage towards the truth], or *parrhēsia* as the right/guarantee to that speech · *logos*. The complementarity · interconditionality of critique and *parrhēsia*, in a word critique=*parrhēsia*. Critique as desubjugation performed through *parrhēsia*, or the weaponization/counter-epistemization of *parrhēsia* which is made possible through critique. The care-taking of the soul secured by *parrhēsia* within this complementary joining is similar but different from the governing of

---

20 Critique p. 47 [words in brackets are differences between the Korean and English translations — Translator's note]

21 Michel Foucault, *Discourse and Truth and Parrēsia*, trans. Nancy Luxon, (Chicago: University of Chicago Press, 2019), 23-24. [Words in brackets are differences between the Korean and English translations. — Translator's note]

the soul by state management's art-of-measurement, and it preserves the insubordinate power of critique by rooting itself in the irreducibility of that difference. When *parrhēsia*—as the art-of-critique against the permanent control system of power-truth, its techniques of taking-care · looking-after life · living, and the cultivation · experimentation · renewal of these techniques—is said to be founded in none other than '*metron*[measure],' '*kairos*[(the contemplation or seizure of) the appropriate occasion to guide and act upon the soul],' and '*krasis*[medical compound for relief and alleviation],' this means it is the technique of counter-measurement[anti-metrētikē], counter-guidance[contre-conduite [counter-leadership (counter-command · counter-steering)], and counter-treatment. This is a technique of self-care in which the people voluntarily led by the control · command of the ship called the state—who are the relay port, the medium · catalyst, of authority— sever · reconstruct the particular organization of power relations by transforming and reestablishing the relations with themselves which are organized under governance's web of relations. This technique—the technique of critique≡*parrhēsia* which points out and reveals the aim · method · tendency · limit · threshold · violence of conjoined power-truth from within that joining—can be read as a kind of art-of-war under the name of 'the emergence · practice of counter-history': "It is, rather, about establishing a right [law] marked by dissymmetry, establishing a truth bound up with a relationship of force, a truth-weapon and a singular right. The subject who is speaking is [...] a subject who is fighting a war."[22] The "aim of the care of self" constructed · accomplished through *parrhēsia*, or in other words, through the "truth's armaments[armed truth]," is a"spiritual armament[armed spirit] constituted by true discourses."[23] The construction and speech of a weaponized truth that neutralizes the truth of disease-control=war/government against the state · market · society · body-infesting pandemic(-like thing); or neutralizes the truth produced · accumulated · archived as part of the process of government; or neutralizes the relations of this life-saving-measures-taking civil-war power. When this is the interest of the 'speaking subject'— the '*parrhēsiastes*'—that speaking subject is none other than the one who carries out war, the subject of a counter civil-war. A warlike technique of life that strengthens the

22 Foucault, *Society Must Be Defended*, 53-54.
23 Michel Foucault, "Paresia"[1982.5], *Damron Gwa Jinsil*, trans. Sim Se-gwang and Jeon Hye-ri, (Paju: Dongnyeok, 2017), 79. These unspoken words, left in the form of a note in the lecture manuscript as things to consider and compare, [These manuscript notes are not included in the English translation of the text. — Translator's note] are connected to the last line of the lecture: "I have tried to show you [a] rather curious figure of *parrēsia*." Foucault, *Discourse and Truth*, 33.

'dissymetry' which cannot be integrated or reduced to the regulatory art-of-government of economics · management, and that inscribes into law the permanent neutralization of art-of-measurement · appropriate-bounds. To put it another way, an art-of-care for 'anti-fascist life' oriented towards the speaking of a 'new law': "if we are to struggle against disciplines, or rather against disciplinary power, in our search for a nondisciplinary power, we should not be turning to the old right [law] of sovereignty; we should be looking for a new right [law] that is both antidisciplinary and emancipated from the principle of sovereignty."[24] The bio-measures power which decides the present political array of the pandemic here is creating · propagating · establishing the legitimacy and justice of violence which adjusts · synthesizes · interrupts the vector of such a new law, within the laboratory of politico-economic disease-control. This, here, is the reason why it is necessary to examine the power and direction, vector and character, of this new law. Following that necessity—the necessity of being lead along by the political forces of the pandemic, and of sculpting an 'outside' corresponding to that position 'inside' those political forces—future citation · distribution

---

24   Foucault, *Society Must Be Defended*, 39-40. [Words in brackets indicate differences between the Korean and English translations — Translator's note].

· investigation will be a process—alongside references to Foucault's "In Defense of Freedom"(1980), "Is it Useless to Revolt?" (1979), "Manual For Anti-Fascist Life"(1977), and his criticism of the pastoral system of obedience[a phrase quoted from Solzhenitsyn's novel *Cancer Ward* in *Security, Territory, Population*]—involving the following question: "How can we designate the type of revolts, or rather the sort of specific web of resistance to forms of power that do not exercise sovereignty and do not exploit, but 'conduct'?"[25]

---

25   Michel Foucault, *Security, Territory, Population: Lectures at the College de France 1977-78*, trans. Graham Burchell (New York: Palgrave Macmillan, 2007), 200. ·

∞ Review

When a Researcher from TK Researches on the heart of TK

- Sociology of Daegu & Kyongbuk
(Choi Jong-hee, Maybook, 2020)

Shin Ji-eun[1]

1. What is wrong with TK?

I started reading the book after I was asked to write the review late in March. Since the beginning of the month, Daegu(Taegu) suffered from COVID-19. The criticism toward the city was harsh in relation to the skyrocketed confirmed cases by the mass infection in Sincheonji Churches. It was just before the 21st election of the National Assembly in mid-April. I stopped reading the book. I thought I could read it after the election. The result of the election was just as I suspected. I wondered. What is

---

1   Shin Ji-eun is professor of Sociology Department in Busan National University.

wrong with the people in Daegu and Kyongbuk?

The author starts the story about her experience visiting Seoul with a friend in 2016 when the country was in an uproar by the political scandal of president Park and Choi Soon-sil. From their accents, a taxi driver noticed that they are from Daegu and asked, "Are the people in Daegu and Kyongbuk alright?", and she was surprised that people do not hesitate to relate the national problem to Daegu and Kyongbuk. At the moment, she said, "I felt ashamed"(10). After the local election in 2018, writer Lee Oisoo mentioned 'politically desert island' about TK region and got attacked by malicious comments. Seeing the process, the author hurt her pride and felt ashamed and bitter. She started if there is particular collective representation in her basic boundaries of life, Daegu and Kyongbuk, compared to other regions.

Besides the author, people living in Korea seem to wonder what is the problem with TK. The author explains it with 'habits of the heart'. Referring to the researches of Robert Neelly Bellah and the cultural sociology of Durkheim as her theoretical frame, she insists that heart includes reason, affection, and mind, and situates particular cultural context and meaning as habits. Therefore, if we study the habits of the heart of a group, we can have an insight into the principle of maintaining the group, long-term development, and so on. Habits of the heart is a 'cultural and symbolic' level, and as a general 'cognitive, affective, moral' being, it includes 'ethical, intellectual' standards.

To know the habits of the heart in TK, the author interviewed people in TK. By listening to their story she can analyze the problem since people form their identity by storytelling. There are ten participants in their fifties and sixties in the book. They are normal people in the older generation, consist of quite identical groups, middle class. She tried to do reflective writing herself, so she wanted to meet people in her generation, and since the habits of heart would be examined clearly through who normal people who had not gotten the opportunities to narrate their life, are chosen. Through their stories, Chapter 1 shows people in TK themselves (it includes episodes about affinity, market, civil society, local community, politics, and religion) and Chapter 2 the language of TK people (shadow language, study language, language for unity, memory language, the language of unconditional) and Chapter 3 the life orientation of TK people (value, norms, goals).

2. Does TK really not reflect on itself?

Reading the book, the question "Why does TK do that?" was solved in a sense. TK has a sense of superiority of making presidents in a row by keeping their faith in each other, and because they have the nostalgia of growing together and want to see the world positively, they agree to the conservative party. Through the book, I could know what does the word 'conservative' means to TK and how are the hearts toward former president Park Chung-hee. At the same time, however, I got a few questions, too. The author predicts that the readers can say "the TK people I know are not like that", or "not all TK people are like that, or people in other regions can be that", so she assumes that the research "does not aim to generalize or acquire a representative through the stories of participants but focus on narrating the mentalities of the place and time that they live as narrators." (31-32) Though considering the intention, I think it is not research on a certain region but a study on the habits of the heart of 'a certain generation of a certain region'. Besides, I wonder more whether the participants of the book really 'live as their habits and do not reflect themselves', as she mentioned?

In "The Analysis of Stories about Civil Society", the author criticizes that as TK people live by their habits they do not reach civil subjectivity yet. They still "use communitarian, dynastic, nationalist language and exclude the language of citizen sphere. Participants of the research do not trust media as a system of communication. The citizen sphere can grow only when the society is democratized enough. [However,] The communitarian habits of hearts in TK inhibit the buds of the citizen sphere to sprout. Not using the language of citizen sphere seeking the general virtue shows that they do not reach to the democratic society yet."(135), according to her. She comments that "if the TK people isolated from the civil society want to escape from this, "they should free themselves from the restraints of social convention and form the active individual to see and reason the social field of their life reflectively."(137) If I summarize it, TK people are not reflective civic subject 'yet', so in TK the civil society does not develop 'yet'.

However, a question about these results comes across to my mind if I heard the stories of participants of the research. Yeo Chung-ran, who calls herself 'progressive conservative', estimates those in politics as 'eloquent alchemists, opportunists' and a group performing by their profits and needs. Nam Hyun-moo, who said he does not know much about the politics but feels antipathy to the extreme behaviors of 'Park Sa Mo', explains that considering the condition of his manufacturing company, there is no reason for not allowing the immigration of foreign laborers. Nam Kye-sik criticizes that though the economy develops and society is democratizing, national assemblymen are not working but using the pork-barreling on the electorate to gain votes. Thought as a citizen can be formed during the process of their work, or they can set or modify their political opinion at home. Creating their opinions about immigrants considering the situation of the working field where they have been for a long time, or thinking about international marriages relating their brother who has not gotten married yet, are those things valueless compared to participating in candlelight rallies or donating civil movement organizations?

"The Analysis of Stories about Politics" is similar to "The Analysis of Stories about Civil Society". The author understands the politics limiting it to the council or political system. The results would be different if she includes content about politics in family and daily life. The author criticizes the language of unconditional in TK people, but in the case of Nam Min-soo, he exactly perceives that TK's voting habit of 'Do Not Ask', the unconditionalism is the reason for disrupting local development.

Also, in "The Analysis of Stories about Local Community", TK people "feel comfortable living with the language of their habits, so they do not try to create a new language. [...] The object of their interaction is limited to the region of Daegu and Kyongbuk, and they do not have many opportunities of communicating with others outside of the community", so she writes "they should expand a new strategy by building the public symbol system for a world of inter-subjectivity between other regions above the

boundaries of TK"(155). However, in the case of Yeo Jae-
seon, when she was asked of her thoughts about being seen
as a 'right wing net loony', she answered, "We should not
be conservative loonies. We should change by time." She
was also "stubborn right" in the past, but changed watching
news and joining social life. How about Yeo Chung-ran,
who compares her son, who is a typical 'Hannam(Korean
man)' and son-in-law who is not, saying "the Hannam in
TK is the worst"? "You know Hannam, right? Those in
Daegu and Kyongbuk are the worst. They try to dominate
women, keep women under their feet. The boy who will
be my son-in-law is not. Do you know why people dislike
TK Hannam? There are too many old men who think the
first son's family as a head family, or a married daughter
is no better than a stranger, and it influences following
generations." (142, 146) As the author points out, "Marriage
is a habit to the old generation. It is unnecessary to reflect
on."(72), but Yeo knows well about which man is good
for a marriage, and what style of a person does the young
woman favor nowadays. That is why she is worried about
her Hannam son.

The research leaves regret at the lack of consideration
of people's complexity, the crack of perception. For
example, let us pay attention to the story of Yeo's son again.
In relation to the candlelight rally, Yeo says, "A friend of
my son went to Gwanghwamun or whatnot, and made his

voice to hit the internet news. My son feels proud of the
friend, who majors in History Education in K- University.
He has a sharp historical sight. My son really feels proud
of it."(214~215) Putting her words together, we know that
her son is Hannam from Daegu, advocating the candlelight
rally. Is it not a new type of man escaping the already made
TK image? There is another person I got interested in.
Yeo Gyong-suk participated in the national flag rally as
she thought it was an important historical event, but she
was 'afraid' that she visited Myeongdong Cathedral and
Deoksugung road while the rally(118). She perceived that
the social situation is meaningful enough to be a historic
event, so she even went to Seoul half-willingly and half-
not, but went to the cathedral for sight-seeing. Those are
voices I want to hear more. If we hear more of the people
who cannot be explained fully with ideology or political
opinion, will it show the sense that there live people same
as us in TK?

3. Is universal language really universal?

Here is the epilogue showing the conclusion of the
book. "The language of the conservative familism cannot
overstep the wall. If we establish a new public symbolic
system and expand the ability of cultural association, it

is possible to use the universal language. Then I wish my cultural collective people to create new narratives escaping the boundaries between regions." (372)

It is similar in the part that the author questions, "Not using the language of citizen sphere seeking the general virtue, does it not show that they do not reach to the democratic society yet"(135), and insists, "they should free themselves from the restraints of social convention and form the independent individual to see and reason the social field of their life reflectively."(137) I wonder what is the independent individual for TK people, and what is the 'universal language' or 'general virtue', or 'democratic society' that the TK people do not reach yet.

According to the author, 'faith' works as justice and cause for people in TK. When it is distorted, any reasonable judgment and rational assessment become difficult. There is an established 'between ourselves' culture like family, and it distinguishes profit and privilege from inside and outside of the group. The TK people are not accustomed to orienting reasonable and individual thinking but internalize outdated cultural structure moving by habits and convention. Then what is the reason cultural structure that TK does not reach yet?

Durkheim's religious sociology examines the fact that society works as a religion. It does not only conform to premodern society. Modern society also makes a number of totems substituting the god in the past and intends unity of its worshippers. Some can say TK's 'totemic worship of Park Chung-hee' is outdated, irrational, and fanatic. However, in our lives, we all experience a change of our lives and realization of their meaning by getting a certain totem. People link to each other as brothers and sisters through the totems, so that they can feel a sense of belonging and create identity. If Park Chung-hee is a totem for TK, for someone else it can be money, idol, or democracy. Viewed at this angle, we may live in a society not as demystified or post-religious as Weber said. In this point of view, TK people perform as their groups' cultural values or personal small and large faith, and it has its own rationality.

I refuse to see TK as an unmodern, irrational condition for a mature civil society 'still'. Do the other regions excluding TK conforms to modern, rational, and mature civil society? Is it true that those living there has grown as an independent individual so they are using universal language and communicating openly with others? Which is more fanatic and dangerous between the unconditional worship of TK people who believe Park Chunghee is the best, and the hate towards TK citizens when there is found carcinogen in the tap water of Daegu, people said 'Inhale cancer-causing substance and kill yourself'?

In the old structure of 'Seoul-universal-superior-liberals' versus 'regional-particular-inferior-conservatives', TK is evaluated not as a region with its own value and individuality but as a status not reached to the universality. I wish the regional specialty of TK would rather be interpreted actively.

4. When a Researcher from TK Researches on the heart of TK

In the prologue, the author talks about the recent pain of experience living between the two worlds. "I live in two worlds nowadays. There fight 'the world of life' dominated by habits and 'the world of the academy' orienting sociological thinking inside of me. I feel perplexed coming to and leave these two worlds deeply involved in my daily life. For almost fifty years, I had not felt that uncomfortable in the cultural group where I am included, but after I joined the academic world it feels awkward to meet people affecting in the living world. [...] Because of the distinct feeling substantial or minute time to time, I feel disturbed and painful in my mind. It is like the two worlds exist entirely by individual."(22~23) The pain goes bigger while the research proceeds. In the epilogue, the author explains again the agony, anger, and irony that she felt.

Usually, in social science, it is said neutral that a researcher steps back and gives an objective statement of the subject. However, it is impossible for a reacher studying humans not relating to the participants. It does not harm the neutrality of research. Rather, a new method or result of the research can be derived when the relationship between a researcher and the participants is reflected deeply. At that point, I felt interested in this research of a person from TK studying the habits of the heart in TK.

People may feel humiliated by the question of what is the basis of the belief that they have advocated. It can be painful to be suspected of the affection for someone who has liked without reason for a long time. It looks too cool to investigate my beliefs like this. However, the fact that we are all linked to others can be realized only through such an inquiry. It is not through the authoritative admission of our belief by tradition, habits, or convention, or not through the gaze to others according to the region of origin or position of the group. This is the reflective life. The author seems to start such a reflection through sociology. She talks about herself, "at the moment of researching habits of the heart and putting me on the subject of the reflection, I am certain that I am already expanding to wider world escaping familial self."(371) Therefore, she seems to hope to share such reflection with TK people. Though I questioned her universalist language quite critically, I fully understand her focus on democracy and more universal values and aspire to the society realizing them. Also, I understand the disappointment of her region.

Not far away from TK, I grew up in Busan. On a wider scale, those two regions are categorized as Gyeongsang-do, Yeongnam areas, and in the recent result of the election, they showed similar characteristics. The author's agony and tension researching on the people in her region are communicated to me so lively. I still feel puzzled. It is because, for me, a direct and frank reaction to TK is not to understand but to criticize also.

My trouble is coming from the thought that I would like to see ordinary people living in life at a narrower distance, almost the same height. I want to trust their perception of history, politics, others, and their insights as it is. TK people may also live through harsh history, and experience the burden of everyday life. They might have met important others, and gotten through a meaningful event of one's whole life. Though it proceeded without a hitch, they must have found the meaning of life and the world, established their own political opinion and philosophy of life. For them it was just hard to express directly, so they seemed not to reflect on themselves.

It must be hard to talk about their idol Park Chunghee in front of children, so they may feel regret of changing world and manage to protect it. When they are heard badly on the subject of their belief and are required to convert even, people feel much distress and revolt. It is the distress as much as when they are got rid of the origin of their existence, even though for outsiders the reason of the belief is a weak illusion. How can we solve this?

A sociologist from TK performed the hard work with both heated and cool-headed criticisms toward TK. People keep asking what is wrong with TK, but we should see if there is any hatred below the question and if those outsiders furnish the universal and reasonable cultural structure well. To argue that TK reflects itself with the universal language about changed period and democracy, nation and society, we should consider the problem of hatred and derision toward TK, and the predictable result of it. Though the political and cultural wall surrounding TK seems too high and thick, if we pay attention to the humanitarian aspect of it, will it not show us the possibility of real communication between the two above the wall?

Beyond the Borders :
The Tragedy of Modern History Forcing Opportunities

- The Survivors
(Ju Seung-hyun, Thoughtpower, 2018)
- I Go To Bookstores Whenever I Feel Strange to Korea
(Kim Ju-Sung, Across, 2019)

Jung Gwang-mo[1]

A person is standing on the border. He/she tries to get in. However, coming in, he/she is criticized to be from the outside. The position thought to be inside can rather be a route to a farther exterior. Nevertheless, those on the border still try not to remain there but to go into or out of.

Korean modern history proceeds in a way of the clear distinction between the inside and the outside, so as the insider lives more inward and the outsider lives more outward, it becomes an easy life. Since nobody would want to be asked as an insider, are you not an outsider, or as an outsider, were you not an insider.

---

1   Jung Gwang-mo is a novelist.

If you are hesitating on the border without satisfied with neither the in nor the out, you will get blamed for an opportunist. People who are in the pivot force those on the border to choose one. Borders are always insecure.

In The Survivors, Ju Seung-hyun says, "Korean Peninsula creates many survivors under the separated system. They still live distorted and harsh life. Without unification, every member of our society may bear fate for a survivor."

A survivor means a person who faces a disaster during sailing or climbing. Ju Seung-hyun is a defector from North Korea. In 2002, a twenty-two years old man who served in the North Korean broadcasting station for psychological warfare escaped to a South Korean guard post. It was five minutes of running but risked his life. In the North Korean area of DMZ, he should evade four lines of wire entanglements with ten thousand volts of high-tension electricity and the compact ambush shelters, various obstacles and wire fences, wide mine zone, and the chase of forwarding acquisition radar. He still believed in free and hope above the dangerous battlefront.

Through Hanawon's early adjustment education for North Korean defectors, he came to South Korean society alive with freedom and hope. There he became a 'surplus human'. He confesses. "I had never been starved in North Korea. It was my first time in South Korea. I had a job interview in a gas station for a living, but they all refused me. There piled local newspapers with job advertisements in my house, but there was nowhere for a North Korean defector."

Ju crossed the death line to come to South Korea, but he had to cross another death line called 'the survival in South Korean society'. The line consisting of 'ability', 'efforts', 'self-development, and 'adjustment' is an elaborate, tough, and inextricable net. Some of the defectors succeed. For around ten years, the author meets those from Hanawon at the year-end party. There is a famous journalist of a big newspaper, a Korean medicine doctor, a government officer, a doctor, and an executive of a middle-grade company who has several sons and daughters. Like Ju, they have fought until today "across a death line, in another death line". Whether by their luck or by their efforts, they are sort of the survivor among the sufferers. They cross the border after the success. They are not succeeded because they cross it. They adjusted to South Korean society and try to settle down. It would be great if such happy ending stories are most in the life of the marginal. Most are not.

The writer calmly presents the reality of defectors. According to the researches of the Ministry of Unification in 2014, the average income of North Korean defectors is 1,460,000won, which is less than half of the average income of workers, and the unemployment rate of North

Korean defectors is four times higher than the average unemployment rate. In 2007, according to a study by Korean Criminal Policy Institute, the rate of victimization of North Korean defectors are 24.3%, which is five times more than the average rate, 4.3%. In 2016, the suicide rate in Korea was 24.6 among 100,000 and it had been ranked at the top of the OECD member states for thirteen consecutive years. The rate is three times higher in North Korean defectors.

In ten years after the defect, the author finished his Bachelor's and Masters and got a doctorate in unification studies. It was a harsh and needy process. The author calmly tells us about his experience of survival, and there is left desperation fighting with the wild tide and holding the edge of the raft. One of his acquaintances studying in university died of stomach cancer, a friend of his hometown studying business in South Korea after graduating from Kimchaek technical university in North Korea, hung himself. One defector who was a teacher works as an assistant to a chef, and one defector who served as a colonel keeps living by part time work in a gas station, and the other who was a doctor was dead from a fall cleaning window as a cleaner.

Economic poverty is not the only death line of North Korean defectors. There waits for them harsh prejudice and discrimination, marginalization. The author says that it is heart breaking to think about North Korean defectors. "We are perceived betrayers in North Korea, and both witnesses of North Korean system and secondary or third-rate citizen in South Korea. In the end, we are escapers but illegitimate children who cannot be acknowledged anywhere." Therefore, a stream of North Korean defectors who turned back to South Korea, where they entered risking their life goes on. They choose to live as a diasporic citizen in a global society but Koreans also blame their choice of diaspora.

People in South Korea do not hospitalize the defectors. They once showed hospitality during the system competition with North Korea. Hospitality is the perception and acts of accepting someone and doing them a favor with no condition. You must treat hospitality in a certain space. Koreans are confined in the extraordinary imagination of us, 'single nation', so we accept the perception and hospitalize only those who came in the imagination on their knees. Not only North Koreans, but we also discriminate against all refugees and foreigners from the third world. We feel hard to think about rescuing a survivor without discrimination. Our eyes are geared towards the values and evaluation of the West and America, and without those values, we are afraid of showing the identity of a Korean. Koreans do not exceed the concept of the modern nation-state and hope our country to be acknowledged by the West and America. It is unnecessary to be approved by those left behind, like defectors and refugees, as we just have mercy on them.

Ju Seung-Hyun is concerned about North Korean citizens aware of prejudice, discrimination, and marginalization towards defectors. Beyond worries, he is afraid of it. "If citizens in North Korea know these facts, their emotion towards South Korea will deteriorate, and they will seriously refuse the unification led by South Korea and give away the ambition to unify."

Why will they choose to live in a unified nation if North Korean citizens still have to live as a second-class citizen after the unification? Would most North Korean citizens turn to survivors and diaspora? It is impossible to encompass more than 2.5 million citizens not embracing defectors of 3,000 around. I want to ask, is it worth living in Korea? What does it mean Korean society not tolerable for defectors? Having suffered unlimited competition since childhood, Koreans are accustomed to live enduring on the edge of a precipice. Then is it not a normal life which reality we call life? We cannot serve others food that we do not eat.

The author also asks why South Korean liberals keep silent on the human rights issue of North Korean citizens and defectors. He points out that progressives who are silent on the issue are not the real progressives. It is problematic to use the human rights issue in North Korea as a tool for aggression to their system and put it to silence as they are a clear zone of human rights. No country is safe for the human rights issue. Unless all nations on earth turn to utopia, human rights problems would not suspend.

The second part of the book arranges survivors in the Korean peninsula by the division, periodically from the 1940s to the 2000s. They are the North West Korean Youth Association, Lee Myung-jun in the novel *The Square*, Lee Soo-geun and Hwang Jang-yeop who were the double agents. Among them, repatriators from Japan who went on the ship Mankyungbong attract attention. From 1959 to 1984, 93,339 people moved to North Korea, a total of 186 times. However, the Japanese government hid the fact that they could not come back to Japan and involved the Red Cross to evade its political responsibility.

The author evaluates the repatriators. "Those who choose repatriation in the 1960s would have embarked Mankyungbong to the North with excitement. However, promises were not kept. Their origin brings disadvantages and stigma as to treat them unfairly on joining the army or promotion in the workplace. Passing the 1990s when distributing system did not work well especially, their situation got worse in a sudden."

The worst living state led the North Koreans from Japan to join the group of defection. Some entered South Korea, and the other went back to Japan through the third country.

North Korean writer, Kim Ju-sung, who wrote *I Go To Bookstores Whenever I Feel Strange to Korea* is the defector and repatriator from Japan. He was born in Tokyo as a third-generation son of a Korean family in Japan. He grew up teased as 'Josenjing' by Japanese friends, and in 1979, in his sixteen, became one of the 'North Korean people' boarding on the repatriation ship with his grandparents. In North Korea, He had to spend his growing season called 'Jjokbari' or 'Jjaepo'. Having worked as a writer in Joseon Writer Association, he defected from North Korea in 2009 and became a South Korean citizen. He is, so to speak, the marginal men between borders.

Let us see his family history. "My grandparents were from Gyeongsangdo. They went to Japan during the colony and I was born there. Because of their ideology, they went to North Korea and I followed. Being a teenage boy, I do not know exactly about any concept of thoughts or system. I just hoped pleasant future in a socialist utopia without prejudice or discrimination. But there is no freedom. There is no hamburger or ramen. In the end, I defected from there and settled in South Korea, where my grandparents are from. Since they left for Japan in the 1930s, it took almost 80 years to be back on the starting point."

When he was asked what was his favorite coming back to South Korea, Kim answered without hesitation, "the thing I like the most is that you can have electricity for 24 hours without blackout, and you can have tap water, besides, it is warm and edible, for 24 hours." For him, 'the taste of freedom' feels like electricity and warm water. As he spends his teenager in Japan, Kim's writing and thoughts are bright and delightful. His way of apprehending South Korea is through 'books'.

Experience is one way to understand the world, and imagination is the second, book is the third. Resources like books and movies represent the real world through a filter. As he perceives through books, South Korea has a backdrop of romanticism. It is far from the frustration shown by Ju in *Survivors*. But why? Is it because Kim's grandparents have lived in Gyeongsangdo, so they are originally from South Korea? Or is it because the electricity and warm tap water are such a material temptation that overpower other inequality and discrimination? Or is it just because of his bright character?

More than his way to approach South Korea through books, it rather interests me to compare the book with the life in North Korea. He was a writer in North Korea, 'the uptown' for us. He explains that literature in North Korea is a kind of propaganda for the promotion of the system that is hard to deviate from the fixed frame. Writers in 'the uptown' are 'professional novelists'. With the salaries paid by the nation, they have to publish works as much as they are decided. For a novelist, it amounts to 2 or 3 short novels in a year, or a middle-length novel in three years. If they do not accomplish their governmental work, they are marked as 'inactive writers' and are weeded out from the writer union. As Kim read Murakami Haruki's *A Novelist as Profession*, he realized that books are written for selling and that in such an outside world like South Korea, it is hard to be a professional novelist.

Reading *The Life of an IMF Kid* by An Eun-byul, Kim Ju-sung learns how South Korean young men live through the period of crisis in 1997. In North Korea, the generation who experienced the disastrous food crisis and famine in the 1990s is called 'jangmadang(market place) generation'. It means a generation who was grown up by the people starting their own business after the governmental supply system was suspended. Kim thinks that 'IMF kids' and 'jangmadang kids' might be the generation who shared similar hardship in different environments but does not compare them deeply. He just introduces an argument that South Korea could succeed such a fast social reformation and economic development as they experienced 'IMF', and throw a light notion that a revolution can be accomplished through the pain.

Reading *A Critical Biography of Jeon Tae-il*, Kim can criticize the history of Korea which he just has respected. After *Why Do We Need Christianity*, he speculates why there are so many churches in South Korea and what can the church do for society. And reading *The Joy of Engineer's Thinking*, he compares poor engineers in North Korea and rich engineers in South Korea.

Kim's understanding of South Korean society through books is superficial. In other words, he is excessively affirmative to South Korea and its people. At least so are his mentions in the book. While Ju Seung-hyun is interested in making North Korean defectors political producers, Kim Ju-sung apprehends South Korea as a political consumer through the external phenomenon. It is not that bad. It is one side of reality apprehending South Korean society supplying abundant electricity and hot water. However, there are diverse ways of political consumption and it includes a road to change the society better as consuming.

Ju's book is full of speculation as to the marginalized, Kim barely considers it. He affirms reality and treats discrimination or exclusion as a condition of the human world rather than criticizing it. Kim faces the life of the marginalized with light and cool affirmation. With his wife having the first Christmas tree, he realizes that "depending on what I have in view, a small tree can bring such a big pleasure." It may be the reason for him adjusting to South Korean society as an entertainer and teacher.

They are all certain ways of life and a North Korean defector can make any choice. I just want to rethink the meaning of the margin and those who are marginalized. The history of life on earth is that of life newly developed and adjusted after being expelled and cornered to the boundary. Fish drove out to the land evolved with its lung. It comes around the land above the water after a drought or the surface going lowered, to be the human ancestor who steps up to land. Birds also choose to fly as the survival on the margin is desperate. Margin is painful but becomes the starting point of the new creation.

The marginalized are also like that. A North Korean defector is a person standing on the border of South Korea and North Korea, but they are standing on keen boundaries inside South Korea. The boundaries pan out across various fields such as economy and politics, exclusion and discrimination, inclusion, and acceptance. Every marginalized man is doomed to a painful life. Through life, the creation crossing a new line across the margin happens. I hope Ju Seung-hyun and Kim Ju-sung's efforts making a new line succeed. Above all, I hope they feel happy in the process. If they are too distressed I am worried of others following them feel hard to put the next step forward. I wish for their peace and good health.

Living in a Disaster :
On the Universal Grammar called Disaster Narrative

- Bunker X in Burim District
(Kang Young-suk, Changbi, 2020)

Kim Dae-sung[1]

1.

Kang Young-suk's *Bunker X in Burim District* throws consecutive questions of what we look forward to from a 'disaster narrative'. For example, it is the expectation such as an aurora coming to seem when all electricity in a city is out, or creation of not hierarchical but mutual aid community between the victim and the helper to bring about a new way of life[2], or expectation to the dramatic change of the world when it resets or disastrous spectacle by a sudden disaster. Lacking in those things, *Bunker X*

---

1   Kim Dae-sung is a literary critic.
2   Rebecca Solnit, *A Paradise Built in Hell*.

in Burim District is quite flat and plain. But also for that reason, it requires to contemplate the changed coordinate of the 'disaster narrative'.

In 2020, the spread of Coronavirus across the world was not just a past broken out temporary but a powerful system subjecting recent life. Though it seemed to make an unwarned outbreak, the disaster sent ceaseless warning signals in our daily life. I would say our life since a certain period has been always with signs of disaster. As the disaster and life are undetachable, the coordinate of the 'disaster narrative' must be changed. Now disaster is not 'there' but 'here' in front of our nose. 'Our nose' is a condition not just referring to the proximity distance but the so-to-speak filter necessary for our survival, which the disaster should pass whenever we breathe. Today's disaster is a 'dispositif' thwarting our life breathing but also allowing us to breathe. If we do not follow the order of life changed by the disaster coming to our nose, we can be quarantined or expelled so it is a condition of survival. Therefore, now the disaster is not a thing to protect against by proper prevention or the object to overcome with an indomitable will. Since it became the field of today and the condition of life.

Everybody lives in the disaster. As the 'disaster in front of the nose' is a dispositif letting or taking the breath, 'disaster utopia'(Rebecca Solnit) and 'disaster capitalism'(Naomi Klein, *Shock Doctrine*) entwine and proceed at the same time. In that entanglement, it is common for the overturned life to be shown by the disaster rather than the life turns over by the disaster. The evidential cases are, frustratingly, too much. The group infection at Daenam hospital in Chungdo, Kyungbuk and substantially high rate of death, the faithful in their twenties sacrificing themselves in Shincheonji religion and Hanmaum apartment where the female devotees lived in the group, the accountants in call centers of each region. Each infected place should be seen as a blind spot of basic rights, not of public health and precautions. Rather than breaking the grund of the world, disaster discloses the covered system and history having deprived and extorted civil rights. It is the reason why we cannot just nod our heads on the argument that people who lose residence by disaster assimilate floaters such as hunters and gatherers and the reciprocal change form(change form D) emerges.[3] Lacking disastrous spectacles and any hope for restoration, Bunker X in District Burim asks why those who are deserted or deprived of civil rights have come to the frontier of disaster.

2.

---

3   Karatani Kojin, *Nature and Human*.

There is no utopia or the Apocalypse in *Bunker X in Burim District*. There no serious event happened or conspicuous tension between the characters, but only presenting a suddenly made bunker and a few people who escaped, and memories and stories about Burim District. The description or explanation about Big One is also presented simply. Since the time is a year after the outbreak of the disaster. there finds little emotion of desperation and eagerness, or few animate narratives of loss and pain led by the disaster. If you search for any exciting factor in the story of life in the bunker going helpless and of trivial tensions at the state of isolation, it is that the government selected Burim District as a contaminated area to focus on immigrating survivors to N city. The government considers the survivors in Burim District as the object of control and management so it tries to transplant a chip on the refugee's skin. Some complain about its one-directed surveillance, others eschew governmental agents not to move out of Burim District. Instead of downsizing the narrative factors of a disaster, each side of life continuing in the emergency seems conspicuous. Throughout the story, it becomes clear not the abrupt acts or struggles in a state of exception but the career of beings living in the bunker.

It is Kang Young-suk's talent to make characters unrelated to each other gather in a place accidentally and share the undistinguished but surely intimate stories leading to unfolding the originality in the commonness. Her career keeping on narrating the stories of those who are left after the disasters such as yellow dust, viruses, drought, flood, earthquake, and hurricanes, shines in her 'power of transformation' creatively and amazingly changing the seats for mediating the conflict caused by the excrement handling issue to "a contest of storytelling my experience of the earthquake"(148). The stories of a mother who has worked in a textile factory making a wig from her teenage, a foreign wife who disappeared, a disaster reporter who rather feel comfortable in the disastrous field, an ex-assistant in a dance hall in Burim District who now suffers from a rotten foot are not tied to the sites of confession and monologue but revealed as a power 'to make anyone feel for telling something'.

Unlike most disaster narratives hastily proceeding to the phase 'after' the disaster, Bunker X in Burim District takes a method to live out the presence of a disaster. So to speak, rather than presenting the route to escape the ruins and ashes of nothing to be expected, it focuses on polishing how to live in the ash. As "the only way to survive in the ash is becoming one with it"(181), the survival technique in a disaster is similar to the adaptation to the feigning technique of "originally scattering the exterior of human and pretending to not a human"(177). It is not a way of restoring the damage made by a disaster but a technique turning the damage into a condition of life, and it is based on posthumanism. 'I', the narrator in the book who used the nickname 'Yujin', said that "the earthquake leaves a good time to deceive others about myself."(19) 'Hyena', who dreams of "being a disaster actress acting the situation of common people who got damages"(21) grows up as an earthquake actress from the victim in the bunker. This explains that Kang Young-suk's disaster narrative does not aim for 'being (myself)' but focuses on the capability of 'becoming (other)'.

3.

On the ashes, after everything was collapsed by the disaster, Kang Young-suk stares at the mound of ruins. Burim District is not a mark displaying the geographical coordinate of *Bunker X of the disaster* survivors but it is rather an area of truth shown after the entire devastation. Besides Bunker X in Burim District is not a story of 'disaster survivors' but a story about Burim District becoming total ruins after the disaster. The survivor 'I' also makes the most effort in the bunker to rub off and tear up the layer of memory lying in Burim District. It was already being collapsed before the disaster broke up, and now Burim District can finally tell its story after becoming complete ruins. Similarly, the voices of those who were so weak and poor that they had not talked about themselves absorbed in their own work remain as a layer of dirt in Burim District. It would be more effective to construct a disaster narrative focusing on the incidental and flexible singularity of Bunker X, but through the grammar of disasters, Kang Young-suk intends to concentrate on storytelling the place erased in everyone's memory.

Burim District structured as a model description of declined peripheries is not so different from the usual picture of the city made by nation owned industry and becoming hollowed by its rise and fall. Closing, severance, declination is a cliche shown continuously when we imagine a 'region' in Korean society. The value of 'locality' in the book is not only the thing generated by the cliche of the regional representation. As the impossible-looking plan on the thick note which 'captain' gives 'I' when he leaves the bunker, the attitude to imagine the impossible in the ruins' state of exception might be the most progressive power of those living in a disaster. Yet, the fact that the power depends on the familiar system of representation of the region displays the stubborn dignity of images about the region even at the ruins after all destruction.

Of course, it is unfair to judge the description of the Burim District only with the frame of the region. Because it cannot explain the passion of 'I' trying to tell about the declining city that no one remembers clearly in a condition of life hard to even live out a day. In an emergent state as disasters, the power of enduring present is not from the hope to the future. As all foundations of the world collapsed here and we cannot expect tomorrow, there is no more unluckiness.[4] On the site where everything has gone, I would like to read from the act tearing up the layer of time in Burim District not the regression but the power pushing ahead the ruins. Nostalgia is the memory of utopia that we dreamed of without any sleep when we are kids. In *Bunker X in Burim District*, the ruins of Burim District feel like not the ending point of the terminal nor the starting point of the new order, but a knock waking up the potential in a location.

4.

Now, what we are urgent for is not 'the imagination of a disaster' but 'the realization of a disaster'. Since a long time ago, the world "has been boiled up like a disaster though it is not, and people have suffered a disease and

---

4   Huruichi Noritoshi, *Happy Young Men in the Nation of Despair.*

committed suicides and shown anger."[5] Therefore, rather than imagining the disaster, we need to hone and adjust to the technique of living there. Jo Jung-hwan once said about the 'labor literature' considered as the product of the certain period that in the capitalist system indistinguishable between life and work "labor overlaps with the capital from above and life from below so "ironically there comes to a situation having no literature other than the labor literature".[6] It feels like *Bunker X in Burim District* gather all the characters omnipresent at the disasters in Kang Young-suk's novels in the bunker of Burim District.[7] They seem to hone the way to live in the ashes rather than escape the ruins and ashes. Because of Corona Virus, it is possible to temporarily set the social distance but it seems impossible to detach from the disaster. Therefore nowadays disaster narratives cannot be contracted to a feature of the genre or the subject. It is the universal grammar of nowadays.

---

5   Kang Young-suk, "Disaster Tour Bus" *On the Black in Red*, Seoul: Monhakdongne, 2009, p.107.

6   Jo Jung-hwan, "The Reality of Labor Literature and the Bioliterary Prospect", *The Literature of Kairos*, Seoul: Galmuri, 2006, p.187.

7   The names 'Yujin' and 'Hyena' are also used in her other novels.

translator/Dohee Kang
Dohee Kang is a literary researcher and translator. She received her
master's degree with a study on children's life-writing and she is doing
her doctoral studies at Seoul National University. Currently, she manages
writing class 'Keoreum' and writes columns in Hankyoreh newspaper.

translator/Seth Chandler
Seth Chandler holds an MA in Korean Literature from Seoul National
University, and studied translation at the Literature Translation Institute
of Korea. With co-translator Kim Jinah, he was awarded the 45th *Korea
Times* Modern Korean Literature Translation Award for fiction. His
poetry translations have appeared in *chogwa* webzine and as part of the
'Yeok-si: Multilingual Poetry Reading' series hosted by LTI Korea.

Literature/Thoughts Vol.1
Power and Society

초판 1쇄 발행 2021년 8월 25일

발행인 강수걸
편집인 구모룡
편집주간 윤인로
펴낸곳 산지니
등록 2005년 2월 7일 제333-3370000251002005000001호
주소 부산시 해운대구 수영강변대로 140 BCC 613호
전화 051-504-7070 | 팩스 051-507-7543
홈페이지 www.sanzinibook.com
전자우편 sanzini@sanzinibook.com
블로그 http://sanzinibook.tistory.com

ISBN 978-89-6545-740-4 03800

* 책값은 뒤표지에 있습니다.